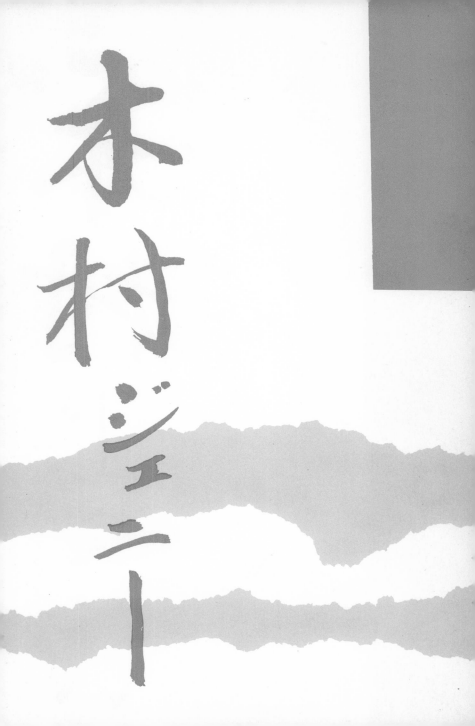

木村ジェニー

JENNY KIMURA

Jenny Kimura

by BETTY
CAVANNA

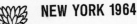WILLIAM MORROW
AND COMPANY

NEW YORK 1964

To my young friend,
Nobuko.

Jenny Kimura

❀ ONE

Gently—almost wistfully—the kneeling girl traced with her forefinger the gilt initials stamped into the leather trimming of her new plaid canvas suitcase. *J.K.S.* The gesture gave her an identity, a sense of being an individual, a person. This would have been heartening if it had not been rather frightening. For the first time she came to grips with the fact that this marvelous journey for which she was packing was no longer just a Cinderella dream. It was about to become a reality.

Jenny Kimura Smith, who had never flown in a plane before, and whose sixteenth birthday had just been celebrated by her family and friends with all manner of going-away presents, was about to take a jet airliner from Tokyo to the United States. She was to visit her paternal grandmother, for whom she had been named but whom she had never seen, and she was going to be away from home for an entire summer —more than three months.

She wanted to go. Of course she did! She wanted to travel to America very much indeed. It would be a thrilling, altogether novel experience, and she was envied by every girl in her class at school.

Yet why did her finger pause on the letter S, and why did she hesitate and stare at it so pensively? Was there an element of alarm in her expression? Had she assumed a joy she did not actually feel? Nonsense! Jenny Kimura was not given to introspection. By nature she was adventurous. She was going to have a wonderful time!

Quickly, in the manner bred into countless generations of Japanese women, she rocked back on the balls of her feet and stood upright. The strong muscles of her legs allowed her to rise with no effort, yet she was not aware that the motion was graceful. It was something she did without thinking, since much of her time was spent either on her feet or on her knees.

Not that the Smiths lacked chairs. The family living room was arranged in Western style, with a sofa and standing lamps and furniture in which Jenny Kimura's American father could be comfortable. The dining room was called "modified Japanese," with flat cushions for seats, and with an open pit dropped into the floor under the low, black-lacquered table. While Jenny Kimura's mother could kneel for hours without becoming tired, her father arose groaning after five minutes in such an unaccustomed position. The well for his feet had been built as a compromise.

Because a house belongs primarily to a woman, Jenny Kimura had been raised in the Japanese manner.

12

While she spoke her father's language fluently, she thought in Japanese and felt like a Japanese. This was quite natural, because she had spent all of her life in Tokyo.

"Jenny!" Her mother's voice, raised to a trill, called from the front of the house. "Yukari is here to see you."

Sliding quickly into the slippers she wore in the corridor, Jenny hurried to greet her best friend who had come to bring her a farewell present.

"I'm sorry I was ill on your birthday," Yukari apologized, as Jenny Kimura ushered her into her bedroom. She held out a prettily wrapped package. "This is a small thing that perhaps you may find useful on your journey."

Still another gift! Jenny thought fleetingly of her father's dire warnings that her luggage would be over the weight allowed in economy class. But fortunately this present was light. She thanked Yukari warmly and knelt to unwrap the parcel, which contained a diary bound in dark red leather, with her name stamped on it in gold.

"Oh, how pretty!" she exclaimed. "And look, it matches my suitcases. See!"

The red was indeed the background color of the plaid, and at this Yukari was especially pleased. Her black eyes lighted and she nodded her head in agreement, her short straight hair swinging gently against her cheeks. "I am so glad," she murmured. "But you please must also write letters, remember? I want to know all about everything." Yukari lowered her voice to a whisper. "Especially about American boys."

"Suppose I don't meet any?" Jenny asked teasingly.

"Oh, you will meet them," Yukari predicted confidently. "The magazines from the United States show boys and girls together all the time."

Jenny frowned slightly. "My mother says American girls are too preoccupied with such things and warns me against them, but I'll write to you. I promise." Suddenly Jenny Kimura had a premonition of homesickness, because leaving her best friend was almost worse than leaving her family. As she carefully folded the paper in which the diary had been wrapped she kept her eyes downcast, not wishing even Yukari to know that she had any qualms. "I'll also write in my new diary, every day."

The two girls, who both happened to be wearing dark skirts and white blouses, looked almost like sisters as they knelt opposite one another on the *tatami* mat. Morning sunlight streamed through the opened sliding doors of the bedroom, highlighting their shining black hair and the soft curves of their cheeks. As though she were lifting a burden, Jenny Kimura suddenly raised her arms and swept her long hair up from her neck, looking up again and smiling. "I wanted to cut it," she murmured ruefully, "but Mother won't let me. Do you suppose all the girls in the United States will have short hair?"

"I don't know," replied Yukari, "but I agree with your mother. I think long hair is becoming to you."

Jenny Kimura twisted around to examine her reflection in the mirror hanging on the opposite wall, and wondered how she would impress the grandmother she had never seen. Her skin was fairer than Yukari's, her eyes larger, though still almond-shaped, tilting impishly upward at the outer corners. She knew that it was improper to feel pride in her appearance, but she couldn't help realizing that a certain animation in her expression made her much more vivid than most of the girls who were pure Japanese. She laughed, then shrugged in a manner acquired from her father. "I just hope the Americans will like me," she said. "I hope they won't find me—odd."

"Odd? Nonsense!" Yukari was indignant. "They're bound to like you. Everybody does!"

"Thank you. Thank you very much!" Jenny Kimura turned back and accepted the compliment gracefully. She was touched by such loyalty, which routed most of her doubts and made her bubble with excitement once more. "Do you want to see my new clothes?" she asked.

"You know I do!"

One by one Jenny Kimura brought her dresses from the closet. There was a blue sheath, bound in white braid, with a short jacket to match; a full-skirted pink cotton; a creamy linen, cut on simple, straight lines. About each one Yukari exclaimed enthusiastically. "Where did you ever find such lovely clothes?" she asked.

"My mother made most of them," Jenny replied proudly. "I found the ideas in the pages of *Seventeen* and in advertisements in *Vogue*, and Mother copied them."

"Why, she's an artist!" Yukari exclaimed. "They're

15

much prettier than anything you could have found in the department stores."

Jenny Kimura thought so too, but she was glad to have her judgment confirmed. The girls discussed which outfit would be most suitable for wear on the plane, considered the occasions on which Jenny would need a party dress, and questioned in lowered tones the advisability of taking along a summer kimono.

"I don't want to," Jenny Kimura said, "but Mother insists. She says my grandmother will surely expect me to have a kimono for special occasions in the States."

"What is your grandmother like?" Yukari asked. "Have you a picture of her?"

"Just a very old one—taken before I was born. I'll get it from my father's desk." Jenny Kimura went to fetch a faded photograph in a silver frame, which showed a slender, fluffy-haired woman leaning on a stone wall and laughing.

"Is she very blond?" asked Yukari.

"She was, I think. Like my father. Though now that she is old I suppose her hair is gray."

"Is she so very old then?"

"She must be. This picture was taken before Daddy and Mother were married. My Japanese grandmother was sixty years old last January, and I know my American grandmother is still older than that."

Yukari looked thoughtful. "Oh, then you will be spending much of your time in the house when you visit her," she murmured, as though she were no longer quite so confident that Jenny would meet many boys.

"Or will someone take you around to see the United States?"

"I don't know," Jenny Kimura admitted. "I can't really imagine what it will be like." This was true. Even though she had read innumerable American books and looked at quantities of pictures she still couldn't visualize a country so vast—a great continent hundreds of times the size of all the islands in Japan. She knew that her grandmother lived in Kansas City, which was just right of center on the map of the United States. She knew that one month of the summer would be spent at an inn on a squiggle of ink running out from the eastern seaboard, a place called Cape Cod. But how long it took to get from one place to another, or whether the customs differed in these two spots, as they did in Tokyo and Hokkaido—this she did not know.

Lying in bed that night, Jenny Kimura felt her heart thumping against her chest. Gratitude for her great good fortune was mingled with a certain fearful anticipation. Tomorrow her packing would be finished, and in the evening her parents would drive her out to the airport and see her off on the plane.

She tried to imagine what the house would be like after she had gone. Quieter, she thought. Her mother would no longer have to say, "Hush, Jenny. Listen to the lark in the garden. Hasn't he a beautiful song?"

When she was gone the birdsong would be uninterrupted. When she was gone her mother would be here alone all day. For the first time Jenny Kimura rather

17

wished she had a brother or a sister to leave behind for company. It was a rare and responsible thing in Japan to be an only child.

Once she had asked her father, "Aren't you sorry you don't have a son?"

"Not really." He had pulled her to him and hugged her in his ebullient American manner. "You're quite enough for me."

But Jenny Kimura knew that her mother regretted that there was no son in the household. Right after her daughter's birth the doctor had told her that she could have no more children, and for this reason her family name, Kimura, had been added to the name Jenny, to pay honor to the Japanese grandparents, who would have expected such a gesture had the child been a boy.

A cloud crossed the pale moon shining above the bamboo-fenced garden outside the bedroom door. It was as though the thought of the Kimura family had made the night less bright. Jenny had never quite understood this troubling business of the strained relationship between the Japanese grandparents and their disobedient daughter, who had refused the husband presented by the marriage broker and chosen an American instead.

Jenny knew her mother's parents only slightly. Once a year, on New Year's Day, the Smiths went to the country village where the Kimuras lived and paid their respects, but these were the only times Jenny had ever seen them, and for as long as she could remember she had felt they were formal and cold.

18

"Why?" she had asked her mother when she was still a child. "Why does my grandfather treat us as though we are strangers in his house?"

Her mother looked sad and troubled, but she tried to explain. "My parents cling to the old ways," she said. "They are landowners, and in their village the peasants who tend the rice fields look up to them as very important people. It is an embarrassment to them—a tragedy even—that I married a foreigner."

Jenny Kimura was incensed. "But Daddy's so *nice!*" she cried. "I should think, once they got to know him, they'd be pleased!"

"They'll never get to know him," her mother said, shaking her head. "They won't allow themselves to."

Later Jenny Kimura learned that her Japanese grandparents had refused to attend their daughter's wedding. It had been a great concession that they had sent their eldest son as a representative of the family. Even this had been frowned upon in the village, where it was thought that an erring daughter should be banished from the house forever, and not even be received on New Year's Day, when the peasants came to pay their respects.

But even though they were treated with distant formality, the Smiths went by train on the first of each year to the district in the rice-growing region where the Kimuras lived. From the station they walked on a narrow path through the rice paddies and along a street between thatch-roofed cottages to the gate that led to the landlord's house. Often the dirt road was frozen, and sometimes there was snow on the ground.

19

Few people were about, because on New Year's Eve, the Great Last Day, there had been feasting and celebrating until midnight, when the gongs in the Buddhist temples had been rung 108 times. Now most of the men were sleeping off the effects of *sake*, combined with the heavy rice dumplings called *mochi*.

Across the top of the gate to her grandfather's garden, Jenny remembered from her earliest visits a rope stretched and hung with strips of white paper. It was a custom held over from the old days, a kind of taboo rope, her father explained, supposed to put the house off limits to evil spirits.

At the front door, heavy and black with age, were a pair of small pine trees and, in back of each, three stems of bamboo. The decorations never varied, and were as traditional as the American Christmas tree the Smiths had annually in their living room. The evergreen tree denoted long life; the straight bamboo stood for constancy and virtue. Inside there were other symbolic decorations—fern leaves with many fronds, suggesting expanding good fortune for the coming year, and small papier-mâché lobsters with curved backs, promising old age.

When she was about four years old, too young to be aware of strained relationships in her mother's family, Jenny Kimura had been unable to keep her small hands off the lobsters. As it came time to leave she had run to her grandfather and begged, in Japanese, "Please, may I take this home?"

Even now, lying snug in her room on this late-spring night, Jenny could recall the shock she had felt when the unsmiling old man shook his head in refusal. He had looked beyond the child to her mother, and said coldly, "She is like you, Midori; she would take away my old age."

"Never mind. Daddy will buy you a toy lobster," Jenny's mother had said, trying to comfort her as they walked back to the station. But then everyone had pretended to forget, because, of course, a toy lobster wouldn't have been the same.

Now that Jenny Kimura had reached an age of understanding, the Smiths shared the annual visit as a family obligation. Each of them hoped the grandparents would finally relent, but as the years passed the estrangement remained, and it seemed unlikely. It was one of the sad but inevitable things in life the Smiths did not talk about. Each Christmas Midori wrapped the usual New Year's gifts with a leaden heart.

Very gradually Jenny had become aware that the Kimuras were not alone in their prejudice. "My own mother was just as quick to censure," her father had explained after a particularly trying New Year's visit. "She has never really recovered either from my marriage or from my brother's death." Yet he didn't speak bitterly, then or later, when he talked to Jenny about her visit to Kansas City. "Richard was Mother's favorite," he said. "He had personality and brains and forcefulness, all qualities she greatly admires."

"But so have you!" Jenny cried defensively.

"Watered down. Besides, I have one quality your grandmother doesn't admire. I'm unconventional. Who ever heard of a man who'd choose, of his own free will, to marry a Japanese girl, settle in Tokyo, and make a hobby of raising bonsai trees?"

They had both laughed, because the description sounded so utterly normal. Then Jenny's father had said, "You'll get along, chicken. Just be yourself and she'll grow to love you, but it may take a while."

No wonder the gifts Jenny was to take to her American grandmother seemed almost as difficult to choose and make ready as the annual New Year's presents to the Kimuras. There were long consultations on what to buy, with her mother troubled by the responsibility, because she considered these tokens of Jenny's arrival of immense significance.

"What does your mother enjoy, Gordon? How is her home furnished?" Midori wanted to do the right thing.

Glancing up from the newspaper he was reading, Jenny's father looked vague. "She likes antiques," he said finally. "She came from Philadelphia, you see."

Midori's eyes widened. "Antiques? What dynasty?"

Her husband burst into laughter. "American antiques!"

This confused both Jenny and her mother. How could there be things of antiquity in a country that was less than 500 years old? But they searched the shops, and finally decided on an Imari bowl, made by some skillful craftsman of the Tokugawa period. Packed in tissue, wrapped with beautiful handmade paper, and tied with colored raffia, it rested right now on Jenny Kimura's bureau.

She raised herself on one elbow, trying to see the

package in the darkness, wanting the reassurance that it was really there, because this was something tangible she would carry in her hands when she set forth across the world. The cloud had passed. The moon flooded the small garden once more, touching the stone lantern and the green leaves of the azaleas, now past their time of flowering. It was quite late, and silence had descended on the street outside the fence. Jenny Kimura stretched and lay back on her pillow, tense with excitement, too tired to sleep. Then, from a house a few doors distant, owned by a musician who taught his pupils the art of playing the *shaku-hachi,* the Japanese bamboo flute, came a thread of silvery sound.

Jenny Kimura listened, thinking that when his pupils played it was a torment, but when the teacher played to himself, as he did all too seldom, it was sheer delight.

She closed her eyes against the moon's shine and began to relax as the flutist played on. Finally, on her last night at home, it was the fluid, sweet sound of an old Japanese love song that lulled Jenny to sleep.

❦ TWO

Morning came, not with trumpets to herald a special day, but just as usual, with the sounds of a familiar barking, then the scratch of Gordon Smith's sandals on the gravel path of the garden, the rattle of a released chain, and the soft patter of a little dog's feet as he came to leap upon Jenny's bed.

It was a great concession that she was allowed to have her pet in the house. Because shoes are not worn on the *tatami,* most Japanese house dogs are trained to stay in the small entrance vestibule called the *genkan,* but Jenny Kimura's father, being an American, thought this was overfastidiousness. When he had bought Togo as a present for his daughter's fourteenth birthday, he had argued the point with his wife.

"Now, Middy," he urged, using the nickname by which he always called her, "it isn't as if a *chin* were a big dog like an *akita.* Why, this fellow will only weigh five pounds full grown. He won't even be as big as a cocker spaniel, and that's considered practically a lap dog in the United States."

Now Togo was more than two years old, but he still raced to his mistress like a puppy the moment he was released from his chain. A bundle of black and white fur landed against Jenny Kimura's chest, a cold nose burrowed under her ear, and she cuddled the little dog to her, laughing even while tears rose in her throat at the thought of leaving him.

Then she held Togo off, both hands around his wriggling body, and commanded him sternly, "You be good while I'm away. No slipping through the gate. No running in the street! Understand?"

"*Wan!*" barked Togo, as though he were replying. "*Wanwan!*" Jenny chuckled, because her father always said that Japanese dogs barked in Japanese. American dogs, he claimed, said "Bowwow."

There was the soft sound of a screen sliding on waxed runners, and Jenny's mother stood at the entrance to the bedroom, one slender hand pushing gently at the *shoji,* her eyes still narrow from sleep. She smiled a good-morning even before she spoke, and Jenny thought, as she often did, how pretty she was, with her slight, slender body, her oval face and smooth black hair. She looked delicate, perhaps because her shoulders were sloping, not square and robust like her daughter's; yet she did not tire easily and there was remarkable strength in her hands.

"Have you been awake long?"

Jenny Kimura shook her head. "Just a few minutes.

But," she admitted, "I had a hard time getting to sleep last night."

Her mother nodded in understanding. "Come eat some breakfast."

"May I come in without dressing?"

Midori hesitated, then relented. "I guess so, today."

A few minutes later Jenny Kimura, wrapped in an old summer kimono she used as a robe, slipped into place at the low table opposite her father, who looked up from his coffee and grinned amiably. "You look all Japanese this morning, kitten," he chuckled. "I'd give a good deal to see my mother's face when she first catches sight of you."

This was a remark so purely American that Jenny Kimura didn't know how to interpret it. At another time she would have asked probing questions, but today her mind was buzzing with too many other important matters to pay much heed. She toyed with her rice, stirring it with her chopsticks, and nibbled at a pickle, then took a sip or two of green tea. Her breakfast was like her mother's, but her father always had orange juice, coffee, and toast, along with a couple of eggs.

Today, to tempt an appetite made skittish by anticipation, Midori brought Jenny Kimura an egg scrambled with butter and sugar, but even this she barely touched. "I'm just not hungry," she apologized. "I'm too excited to eat a thing."

Her father grinned. "Let her alone," he suggested. "She can live on her puppy fat for a day or two."

But at this remark Jenny Kimura bridled. "I'm not fat!" she protested. "I only weigh a hundred pounds."

It was typical of the Smith household that the bathroom scales on which Jenny weighed herself were American, while the lacquered bowls in which much of the food was served were Japanese. Jenny Kimura and her mother could use a knife and fork quite as well as they could use chopsticks, and the table appointments were varied according to the food served. It never occurred to any of them that this was unusual until Jenny brought home a school friend who had never encountered Western ways. Laughing, Gordon Smith had said afterward, "We're very lucky people, actually. We have the best of two worlds."

Breakfast over, Midori helped her husband into the jacket of his tropical worsted suit, reaching up on tiptoe while he, out of habit, bent his knees. Jenny Kimura watched them in affectionate amusement. Her father was so tall and broad, so fair and ruddy, that he made her mother seem especially tiny and doll-like. She knew that out of a custom never broken, even on especially busy mornings, her mother would accompany her father to the gate, hand him the briefcase he usually brought home from the bank in the evening, and say a last good-bye. This morning she added, "Come home early if you can, Gordon. Jenny will be paralyzed with anticipation."

The *kaseifu*—day servant—came and cleared the breakfast dishes, looking curiously at the daughter of the house from under her lashes, as though she were abashed at the thought of a young girl's being allowed

27

to go so far away. It gave Jenny a feeling of pride, a sense of being somewhat superior, and an impetus to complete her packing, which she had been putting off.

Togo followed her back to her bedroom, frolicking at her heels while she went from cupboard to suitcase, folding her clothes in orderly fashion so that her mother would not consider her careless, and tucking in corners of the luggage, here and there, the presents her school friends had brought her—a packet of ribbons to tie back her hair, some handmade letter paper, a painted scarf, a string of beads.

The rain, which had mysteriously stopped last night, started again. The music on the rooftops would probably continue all month, and then would come July, with its bright sunshine and oppressive heat. It seemed strange to Jenny to realize that she would be far away from Tokyo, in a place with a climate she couldn't imagine, even though her father had tried to tell her what it would be like.

Packing took less time than she expected. Long before noon she was finished, in spite of the hindrance of Togo, who kept nipping at her ankles and begging her to play, as though he suspected something unusual was afoot and wanted to reestablish the status quo.

"Come here!" Picking the dog up, Jenny fondled him, murmuring endearments, then tucked him under her arm and went to look for her mother. She found her in the dining room, kneeling on the *tatami* in front of a flower container and a few freshly picked roses, considering the dewy buds with a pensive look in her eyes.

She didn't speak and Jenny didn't disturb her. Kneeling some distance away, she cradled Togo against her chest and watched quietly, as she had a hundred times before. She was contemplating a perfectionist, who had studied the art of flower arranging under one of the great masters of Japan, and Jenny knew that her mother could place a spray of cherry blossoms, half a dozen chrysanthemums, or these few roses in a picture that was like a poem. Someday, she thought to herself, I'd like to have Mother's skill. She knew, without special pride, that she had inherited some of Midori's natural artistic talent, but not until she could study under a good teacher would she have a truly educated eye.

After about twenty minutes, when she was apparently satisfied with the composition, Jenny's mother arose and carried the vase of flowers to the alcove, placing it slightly off center in front of the *kakejiku*—the long scroll that is always part of the simple decoration of a Japanese room. This particular scroll was a favorite of Jenny's. With delicate brushwork the artist had, in a few lines, presented a view of mountains rising above a bamboo wood. Her mother loved it too, because it had tranquility, a virtue she prized highly, both in her arrangements of flowers and in her own life.

"That looks beautiful!" said Jenny in English, because she wanted to express the ultimate in admiration, and this would have been unseemly in Japanese.

Her mother glanced over her shoulder, smiling gently. "The first blossoms," she replied, disclaiming

29

any special prowess, "are always the most graceful, don't you think?"

With a start, Jenny realized that it was incredible that they should be spending their time like this, chatting casually about roses, in the last few hours before she would set off on a trip nearly halfway around the world. Impulsively, she cried, "Oh, Mother, I'm getting scared. I wish you were coming too."

Midori shook her head. "It wouldn't do. It's better that you go to your American grandmother alone. I wouldn't have enough English and she would find me difficult." She paused, then added almost wistfully, "Perhaps someday your father and I will travel, if he gets sent back to the States on business, or when he retires. I should like to see France and England as well as America."

Jenny Kimura's eyes widened. It had never occurred to her that her mother had any desire to see the world, although she knew it was the dream of almost every one of her schoolmates. It made Midori seem like a different person, an individual full of unsuspected depths. Then, on second thought, Jenny realized that her mother had always been a woman of courage. Otherwise, she would not have had the temerity to break away from her family's discipline and marry an American.

Yet it was still remarkable that a Japanese wife should express such a hope. The remoteness of these islands made world tours available to the very rich only. It was difficult to take money out of the country, and women rarely accompanied their husbands. Their place was in the home.

But very gradually this situation was changing. Jenny Kimura, because of her mixed parentage, had some advantages over her friends, one of which was this windfall from her American grandmother—the astonishing invitation to spend the summer, and the check to cover her airplane fare. No wonder she was the envy of her classmates, and no wonder trepidation struggled with anticipation as the time approached.

Lunchtime came and went, the rain slowed to a drizzle, and Jenny Kimura, unable to face her mother's suggestion that she take a nap, decided instead to get Togo's leash and go for a walk. Anything to pass the time, which at first had raced with breakneck speed, but now dragged as though each minute were an hour.

Outside, with Togo pattering along at her heels, Jenny turned instinctively in the direction of the Keisen Girls' School, where she had been a pupil from her junior-high-school days. From the ditches along the roadside came the subdued sound of flowing water, and overhead a misty sun nearly showed itself through oceans of little raindrops suspended in the sky. The camellia leaves, peeking over bamboo fences, gleamed as though they had been polished, and small pools of water shone like mirrors, upon which Jenny's image appeared tremulous. The scene was very familiar, but today especially dear, since she would be leaving it all behind.

Beyond the fences of the school there was birdlike chatter. Children were racing around the yard, jumping rope and playing with volley balls and basketballs. The windows of the old buildings were open, and inside Jenny Kimura could see classes of high-school pupils, and she knew just where she would have been at this hour, had she not been going away—in math class, trying to comprehend the intricacies of algebra.

She breathed a sigh of relief, feeling very lucky. How wonderful to be released from school in early June! How much more fun she was going to have than poor Yukari, who would have to sit through the rainy season, when her fingers stuck to each book and every paper, longing for summer vacation, which wouldn't start until July 21.

It was Yukari, of all Jenny's classmates, who had given her a feeling of high adventure when her grandmother's invitation came. To Yukari such a journey was unthinkable, because she had been raised within the framework of a very strict family system, a relic of the old Japan. In her household she was the youngest daughter and, therefore, the least important member. Her grandmother, who lived in the house, had drilled her in the belief that only the elder brother was of enough consequence to be allowed to express opinions. For a girl the greatest virtue was submission. Her duty was to make herself useful and agreeable to the men.

Jenny didn't enjoy going to Yukari's house, because the regimen made her uncomfortable. Accustomed to the free and easy atmosphere of her own home, she repeatedly committed small indiscretions or was unconsciously rude, being aware only when the grandmother glanced at her sternly that she had spoken too forthrightly or laughed too loudly.

For her part, Yukari treated Jenny Kimura as though she were a rare bird, uncaged and exotic. The fact that her father was American made her especially fascinating, and Yukari had hovered around the fringes of Jenny's life for years, until she had become almost indispensable. Now, standing before the school gate and glancing up at the classroom windows, Jenny wondered whether she should wait until the 3:30 bell rang, signaling the close of the afternoon session, so that she could walk home for one last time with her friend. But the good-byes said yesterday supposedly had been final, and this would be only an anticlimax. Tugging at Togo's leash, she turned away.

The sky had darkened again. Veils of mist were caught in the foliage of the trees, and pearls of water trembled on every roadside leaf. Tonight the frogs would be croaking in the rice paddies, and she—she would be soaring above the ocean like a giant bird!

A shiver ran down her spine. Jenny Kimura suddenly felt very Japanese. She was passing a *torii*, in ancient times a perch for sacred birds, but now the gate to a Shinto shrine, and on an impulse she turned in. A shady avenue was flanked by tall crytomeria trees, with long needles dripping moisture on the statues set among them. Jenny passed Kannon—a goddess of mercy—and stopped before Jizo, patron saint of children and travelers, here represented as a plump, bald-headed figure seated cross-legged on a rock. She had no offering to add to the bowl of rice and the fading bunch of flowers placed before him, nor did she wish to make one, because she didn't really believe in the superstitions of old Japan. Yet it was customary to ask Jizo's blessing on a journey, and she did so in her heart.

Then, propelled by a force she didn't understand, Jenny passed on under a second *torii* and approached a simple, thatch-roofed shrine. There was no one about but a very old woman, who had stopped at a little font to wash her lips before entering. Jenny, trained by her American father to beware of germs, ignored the font, but approached the altar, where she clapped her hands twice, bowed her head, and wished for a safe journey across the sea. She had some change in her pocket, and as she turned away she tossed ten yen into a small barred receptacle by the door. Then, feeling rather foolish but lighthearted, she hurried home.

Now time, which had been dawdling, raced once more. It was necessary to bathe and dress; then it was time for Jenny's father to come home from the bank. The bags were locked and placed in the *genkan*. Togo was fed and chained in his doghouse. The *kaseifu* left, bidding Jenny a tearful good-bye, which clearly indicated that she never expected to see her again. Finally the family was ready to drive to the airport.

The Smiths were the only ones in the neighborhood who owned a car, which was regarded as a very expensive luxury. On her sixteenth birthday Jenny's father had said, quite casually, "Two more years and

34

I must teach you to drive," and her mother had looked utterly horrified.

"Gordon, what are you thinking of?" she asked. "Japanese women never drive cars—or practically never. Besides, the Tokyo traffic!"

"It's pretty bad," Jenny's father admitted. "But I've managed to survive."

"That's different. A young girl—" Midori broke off, because she saw her husband's eyes twinkling with amusement.

"A young girl," he told her, "usually has better co-ordination than a middle-aged man."

Now, as Jenny climbed into the front seat between her parents, she remembered the promise, and wondered whether her father really would someday teach her to drive. Wisely, she decided this was not the moment to raise the question. All of her father's attention was given to negotiating the dense early-evening traffic, and her mother was murmuring last-minute cautions and instructions to the daughter she was sending so far away.

From Setagaya-ku, the residential section of the city where the Smiths lived, Haneda Airport was a full hour's drive, even under the most propitious conditions. It was necessary to cross the city at an angle in the direction of Tokyo Bay, and since Jenny's father was anxious to avoid the traffic jams of the main streets, he chose a devious route through the winding roads along which two cars could barely pass. Soon the familiar neighborhood in which Jenny had grown up and gone to school was left behind. Residential districts were succeeded by shopping areas, where green-grocers, butchers, bakers, fishmongers, and druggists offered their wares in little shops opening directly onto the narrow street. Here the Smiths' progress was slowed to a crawl, because pedestrians and bicyclists paid no attention to the warning horn. It was the time of day when people were tired rather than wary.

Seated with her hands clasped in her lap, Jenny felt her palms grow damp with nervousness. Her plane was scheduled to leave at eight o'clock, and it was already past six. Would they ever get there in time? "Relax, child," her father told her. But how could she relax, when every minute was more important than the last?

Finally the narrow road met a wide thoroughfare, where signs pointed directly toward the airport. But here the crush was even worse than Gordon Smith had expected. He whistled to himself in annoyance and concern as he edged determinedly into the lines of cars waiting for the red traffic signal to turn to green. Now the car inched forward slowly, and as stoplights halted the car's progress at every cross street it seemed to Jenny that they scarcely moved at all.

Six-thirty came, and the hands of her wristwatch began to creep toward seven. Lights were flickering in the growing dusk, and the car seemed to be advancing with the lethargy of a caterpillar. Jenny bit her lip and swallowed hard, because her throat felt hot and dry. She wriggled uncomfortably, mussing the skirt of her new traveling dress, and looked up at her father,

asking with her eyes for some reassurance. He grinned
down at her as though he was no longer worried at
all.

The next instant Jenny discovered why his mood
had changed so abruptly. A great roaring sound filled
the air, and, looking up, she saw the stream of a rising
jet making twin streaks in the sky. "We're almost
there now, aren't we, Gordon?" Jenny's mother murmured comfortingly, and a few minutes later the car
broke loose from the network of traffic and turned into
the airport approach.

A shiver of excitement made Jenny's spine tingle,
and she gathered herself together, trying to achieve
an appearance of calm, even though her heart was
beating like a drum. Now everything happened very
quickly. One minute her ticket was being checked and
her luggage weighed, and the next she was rushing
upstairs to the departure gate, where a group of her
classmates were waiting to see her off.

Yukari at once broke loose from the group and came
up to Jenny, thrusting a bouquet of flowers into her
arms. "This is from all of us," she explained.

Jenny Kimura hid her face in the blossoms to conceal her emotion. "Thank you," she murmured. "*Domo
arigato.*" It was wonderful to know that her friends
cared enough about her to make this long trip to the
airport. It made her feel cherished, no longer clutched
by fear. She was filled with a tremendous sense of
adventure. Tonight, instead of enviously waving good-
bye to some family friend setting out for Hong Kong
or Honolulu, it was she who was about to fly away in

the plane resting like a leviathan on the tarmac not a hundred yards from where she stood.

When she hugged her father and kissed her mother good-bye, Jenny wept a little from sheer excitement. Then she found herself climbing the steps and turning to look back for the last time. She waved the hand holding the bouquet, and smiled bravely.

"*Sayonara!*" she called. "Good-bye!" Then she went through the airplane door, to be greeted by the sound of soft music and the rustle of passengers finding their seats. Suddenly Jenny Kimura felt grown-up, proud, and very, very lucky. She was going off to see the world!

✺ THREE

Darkness seemed synchronized with the jet's leave-taking. One moment the plane was taxiing along the runway in the dusk and the next it was soaring smoothly up into the night sky. As the pilot turned to get on course, the wing outside Jenny Kimura's window tilted downward, and she got a breathtaking glimpse of the lights of Tokyo spreading out below as far as she could see—millions of miracle lanterns powered by electricity.

Jenny felt a thrill of proprietorship at the sight. This was her home, this largest of the world's cities! Surely even New York could look no more glorious from the sky. Then the wing straightened, the glimpse was gone, and Jenny wondered why she had no sensation of speed in this great aircraft, which seemed as steady and as stationary as a traveling hotel.

A stewardess came by and asked her name and destination, noting them on a typed chart. Another stewardess presented her with a tray containing a light lunch at which Jenny barely nibbled, then came and smiled down at her as she took the tray away. The plane was not crowded, and soon a steward arrived to offer her a small pillow and a blanket and show her how to remove the arms between the three connecting seats, two of which were unoccupied. The aisle lights were dimmed, the drone of the engines became a lullaby, and Jenny curled up under the blanket, shivering slightly from nervous exhaustion and sure that although she wanted to do what was expected of her, she wouldn't be able to sleep a wink.

She closed her eyes, and opened them to daylight. The sun was rising like a torch over the sea, and there was a clink of metal, which indicated that more food was about to be served. Jenny checked her watch. It read only two-thirty, surely much too early for the sun to be shining so brightly, and not at all the hour to be thinking about breakfast. Then she remembered the changes in time, which occur so frequently as modern jet planes fly at high speed toward the rising sun. As the stewardess came by she told Jenny that it was six-thirty A.M. Honolulu time, and that they would be landing in less than an hour. During the six and a half hours the plane had been hurtling eastward over the Pacific it had covered nearly sixty degrees of longitude, and had come to meet the sunrise several hours early.

When she emerged from the plane on Oahu, the strong light blinded Jenny and her legs felt stiff and cramped, but by the time she had been herded with the rest of the passengers through U. S. customs she had recovered her equilibrium and was filled with curiosity.

The waiting room of the Honolulu airport was crowded with the strangest assortment of human beings Jenny Kimura had ever seen. There were hundreds of Americans, wearing leis of flowers around their necks and kissing hello or good-bye. The men were almost invariably dressed in flowered sport shirts, and the women—young, old, and middle-aged—in baglike muumuus, made of gaudy cotton materials. The airport in Tokyo had been crowded but orderly. Here pandemonium reigned. Children ran back and forth, tossing candy wrappers hither and yon on the already cluttered floor. Orchids, jostled from the leis, were nonchalantly crushed underfoot by departing travelers elbowing each other around the ticket counters. Women with artificially colored hair shouted at each other or their offspring, and every once in a while a loudspeaker announced the arrival or departure of an interisland plane. With an hour and a half to spend between landing and takeoff, Jenny wandered through the throng like a waif, torn between fascination and alarm.

Occasionally a beautiful dark-skinned island girl appeared, emerging from the picture like a brilliant figure in a pageant, a fresh red or yellow hibiscus blossom tucked into her shining black hair, and her legs and arms bare. On such a young Hawaiian the muumuu was no longer a shapeless garment. It moved with the wearer, suggesting the sweet curves of her

41

body, emphasizing her strong, straight legs. Jenny Kimura watched these girls with unconcealed admiration. They were like peacocks moving with stately grace among the ill-dressed visitors in a zoo.

But many of the Americans repelled her. The men were so red-faced and brash, the women so inappropriately bedecked, with mink stoles over their arms and bulging straw carryalls crammed with treasures, that they looked like cartoon characters. Nobody glanced Jenny's way. She could move among them as though she were invisible, as indeed she was beginning to feel.

It was a relief to hear her flight called, and she climbed back aboard the friendly jet, anticipating another several hours of sleep. But now the economy section was crowded. Next to her window seat was settled a fussily dressed woman, whose crepey neck and veined hands belied a frantic effort to hold the years in check.

Edging up and down the aisle came a short man with bulging pockets, who seemed to be shepherding not only this passenger but a dozen other ladies of approximately the same type and disposition. Jenny Kimura decided that he must be a tour director, and gleaned that his charges were returning from an excursion through the Sandwich Islands, of which Oahu was a part. "All set, Gertrude?" he asked Jenny's seatmate with breezy familiarity.

The woman nodded, and replied with false cheerfulness, "Everything's okeydoke." Then she moved her ample body as far away from Jenny as possible in the cramped space and mopped her perspiring face.

Takeoff was smooth and swift. Pearl Harbor appeared briefly beneath Jenny's window, looking like a relief map as the plane gained altitude. Then the islands drifted away from her vision and, below, there was only the white-flecked sea. The stewardess checking the passenger list appeared once more, and this time she smiled at Jenny Kimura in recognition, saying, "Miss Smith?"

Jenny nodded, smiling back. "That's right."

"Your name, please?" the stewardess asked the woman beside her.

"McAlpin. Mrs. Gertrude McAlpin." No sooner had she replied than the woman turned to Jenny. "Did I hear her say Smith?"

"Yes," Jenny Kimura said, "that's my name."

"Smith." Mrs. McAlpin appeared to be tasting the syllable on her tongue, as though it were some improbable food that would be difficult to digest. "You look Chinese to me. Where did you get a name like Smith?"

"My father is American," replied Jenny. Then, in order to correct the traveler's strange misapprehension, she added proudly, "And my mother is Japanese."

"Oh, Japanese!" exclaimed Mrs. McAlpin, and subsided to think this over, loosening her seat belt and leaning back against the small pillow she had tucked under her neck. Jenny turned once more to the window, quite willing to drop the conversation, but after a few minutes Mrs. McAlpin said, in a conciliatory tone, "You speak English very well."

"Thank you," Jenny answered politely, but she wondered why this should seem remarkable.

"Tell me," said Mrs. McAlpin, "do they really eat seaweed and grasshoppers, the way they say?"

Inferring that "they" applied to herself, Jenny felt embarrassed. "Certain kinds of seaweed are delicious," she confessed, "and very good for you, my mother says, because they're full of iodine."

"But grasshoppers—ugh!"

Although she had never tasted a grasshopper herself, Jenny couldn't resist murmuring, "Oh, fried, they're quite interesting."

Once more Mrs. McAlpin edged away, or at least redistributed her weight on the far side of the seat, and for several minutes she abandoned the conversation. Then apparently curiosity got the better of her, because she hoisted herself forward again and said confidentially, "There's something else I've always wondered. Do they still bind their feet?"

This time Jenny Kimura couldn't help laughing. "That was in China," she replied, "a long time ago."

"Oh. Oh, I see." Mrs. McAlpin glanced down at Jenny's small black slippers, placed neatly on the footrest in front of her seat, and an expression of relief crossed her pink face. Then she settled back once more and closed her eyes.

Jenny, however, felt increasingly wide awake, as she tried to decide whether such ignorance might be typical of women in the States. Certainly her parents'

American friends in Japan were more sophisticated, but she supposed they were from a different background than this woman at her side. Yet Mrs. McAlpin was a traveler. She had been to the Hawaiian Islands. It would be interesting to know how the trip had affected her. So, when the next meal was served and Mrs. McAlpin roused herself to eat, Jenny reopened the conversation, but instead of asking a direct question, she said, "I should like to see the Hawaiian Islands. They must be very beautiful."

"Oh, they are!" cried Mrs. McAlpin. "We did five of them—Oahu, of course, then Hawaii, Maui, Kauai, and Molokai. That's where the leper colony is," she added with a shudder.

"I've been told there are many orchids in Hawaii," said Jenny.

Mrs. McAlpin nodded. "Growing right outdoors, the way they do in California."

"Which island did you enjoy most?" Jenny ventured.

"Oahu, I think. There was more to do. Though I suppose for those that like peculiar sights the volcanoes on Hawaii are interesting. There are spots where the smoke comes right up out of the ground." Once launched, Mrs. McAlpin went on talking. She described the various hotels in which she had stayed, her disappointment at the congestion of Waikiki Beach, the presents she had bought for her grandchildren.

"You're a grandmother?" Jenny Kimura cried, astonishment overriding her good manners. She was especially surprised, because the dress in which Mrs. McAlpin was traveling was almost as pink as her face.

In Japan grandmothers dressed in gray or black, certainly never in bright young colors like this!

Mrs. McAlpin bridled and preened. "Yes, indeed, dearie," she said. "Three times over." It was obvious that she had interpreted Jenny's surprise as a compliment to her youthful appearance. Then her expression changed, and she confided, "My poor husband died just before the last was born."

Jenny murmured something commiserating, at which her companion immediately brightened. "Oh, it's not as bad as it might be," she admitted. "He left me pretty well fixed, and I can take little trips when I want to, to pass the time. As a matter of fact, in this party all but one of us are widows, and she's a grass widow, if you know what I mean."

"Grass widow?" To Jenny Kimura it was a totally unfamiliar term.

"Divorcey," whispered Mrs. McAlpin, then changed the subject abruptly. "How come you're traveling all by yourself, a little girl like you?"

"I'm sixteen," protested Jenny. "I'm going to visit my American grandmother in Kansas City. It's only on the plane that I'm alone."

"Well," said Mrs. McAlpin. "Well!" For some reason that Jenny couldn't fathom the conversation reached a sudden halt. Mrs. McAlpin inspected her again, as she had earlier, out of the corner of her eye. She seemed to be considering something beyond the possibility of discussion, and retreated behind the pages of a magazine for nearly half an hour. Then she burst forth,

46

as though she could contain herself no longer, "What does your grandmother think of you?"

"We've never met," Jenny admitted with complete candor. "You see, my family lives in Tokyo, and that's awfully far away from Kansas City."

"It certainly is," said Mrs. McAlpin with asperity. She sighed, then added, to Jenny's confusion, "She certainly has a big surprise coming. I'd give a good deal to see her face."

The remark rang a bell somewhere in the recesses of Jenny Kimura's mind. As Mrs. McAlpin subsided once more, she tried to remember who had made a similar comment. For a long time she stared out of the window at the cumulus clouds that covered the sky like a feather bed, then it flashed into her consciousness that her father, amused by her kimono at breakfast, had said virtually the same thing.

Until now Jenny's American grandmother had seemed rather nebulous, a lady in a twenty-year-old photograph, a person from an unknown country, a relative of whom one thought without any sense of reality. Now Jenny began to wonder how the stranger meeting her at the Kansas City airport would appear. Would she walk with a cane, as her Japanese grandmother did? Would she be squashy and pink like Mrs. McAlpin, or thin and bent like the old women of Tokyo? Would she be tall or short, laughing or solemn? Why hadn't she thought to ask her father all these questions? Was it because her father spoke very little of his mother? He talked of his father, who had been in the grain business. Two years ago, at the cabled news of his father's death, Gordon Smith had been very sad, but until this unexpected invitation for Jenny arrived, he had rarely mentioned his mother at all.

Staring out the plane window at the endless sky, Jenny felt as though she were trying to see through a gauze that covered her consciousness and clouded her vision. She felt disturbed, ill at ease, and yet she couldn't have said why. She leaned back in her seat and shut her eyes, thereby managing to dampen Mrs. McAlpin's inclination for further conversation, but in the hours that remained before the plane approached the San Francisco airport she did not sleep.

Walking with the other passengers through the long corridors, which led to an enormous waiting room lined with shops and cafes, Jenny Kimura had a chance to check her watch once more. Again she had to set it ahead to shift from Honolulu time to Pacific time. It was rather confusing to realize that back home in Tokyo it was now only ten o'clock in the morning, while here on the western edge of the United States it was six P.M., eight hours later.

Even more confusing to Jenny was the fact that whereas she had left Tokyo on Wednesday evening, it was still only Wednesday evening here. According to the clock and the calendar, she had flown across the Pacific and landed two hours before she started! But she remembered vaguely that her father had explained this in advance. Somewhere in mid-Pacific she had crossed the International Date Line, where everyone traveling from west to east repeated a day.

This was to make up for all the hours they would lose, one at a time, as they moved eastward around the world.

The last leg of the journey was, of course, the shortest. Once more the character of the passengers changed, and Jenny found herself in a plane full of dark-suited businessmen with briefcases. The stewardesses were kept busy serving drinks, and Jenny was left quite alone. But now she was beginning to feel tired. Air travel had lost its novelty, and she longed only to arrive at her grandmother's house, where she might expect a hot bath and a chance to sleep in a real bed, instead of dozing fitfully in this inclined seat.

Since dusk had turned to darkness there was nothing to see and nothing to do but leaf idly through the pages of an American magazine. The arid state of Utah, with its Great Salt Lake, 30,000 feet below, was quite invisible.

When the seat-belt sign announced the approach to the Denver airport, Jenny pressed her nose against the plexiglass window, searching for lights in the darkness, but she could barely make out the city nestled in its hills, and the snow-capped peaks of the mountains emerged only briefly in the moonlight. Once more the plane roared down onto a runway, paused for half an hour, and rose again. Jenny went back to the lavatory with a toilet kit from her purse. She brushed her teeth, washed her face, combed her hair, put on fresh lipstick, and generally tried to make herself presentable, although her eyes felt like empty sockets and excitement had given way to the weakness of fatigue.

49

Again the *Fasten Seat Belts* light flashed on, and she tried to pull herself together, because she wanted to make a good impression on her grandmother, but she felt very young and timid, and she longed only to get to bed.

The jet dropped lower and lower over the Missouri River. Then it flashed over a high dike, so close that Jenny gasped. There was a jolt, a rush of braking motors, and across the field Jenny could see the Municipal Airport of Kansas City, a low gray building surrounded by the usual complement of arriving and departing planes.

The jet taxied to a stop, and she joined the disembarking passengers crowding the narrow aisle, her purse and the box containing her grandmother's present clutched against her chest. One by one the people ahead of her moved to the door and down into the darkness, ducking their heads and responding variously to the polite good-byes of the stewardess. Finally it came Jenny's turn.

On the steps a hot breeze smote her, making her pay attention to her footing. She followed the broad back of the man ahead to the gate leading to the waiting room, then peered around anxiously, trying to guess which of the people awaiting the plane's arrival could be her grandmother.

A tall, slender woman in a green linen dress moved out of the throng and started toward her, then seemed to hesitate, but again came on.

"Jenny, my dear!" Her voice husky with emotion, the woman called to her, but stopped just short of touching her. To Jenny's intense astonishment she saw that her grandmother—it must be her grandmother!—had burst into tears.

Jenny tried to smile, but she could only stand appalled. Here was a situation without precedent, which she had no idea how to handle. Instead of lifting her face for a kiss or stretching out a hand to be grasped, she reacted in a characteristic way. With grave formality, bending almost at right angles from the waist, Jenny Kimura bowed.

✤ FOUR

Jenny stirred in the strange bed, and her eyelids flickered briefly. She was vaguely aware that it was morning again, but she missed the familiar patter of Togo's quick feet, the greeting from his damp tongue curling on her neck. She felt languid, still drugged with exhaustion, then very slowly awakened to a consciousness that this was not Tokyo. This was Kansas City, U.S.A.

Fatigue had blurred her mind last night, making her incapable of absorbing distinct impressions. She had transient memories of the dark faces of Negro porters at the airport, of a fast taxi ride through empty city streets, of a carpeted hall and curving stairs in a house that seemed more like a hotel than a home, and of a woman in a green linen dress who had wept— why?—then greeted her with solicitude mixed with an emotion that might have been either tenderness or pity.

Pity? But why pity? Had she looked so very tired then, or had she not been presentable? Jenny's mind hesitated momentarily on each possibility, then turned to something far more immediate, curiosity concerning her new surroundings.

Suddenly alert, she sat up in bed, a four-poster with a crocheted canopy, which reminded her of an illustration in *Little Women*. (Hadn't Meg slept in a bed like this?) She was immediately aware of an unnatural chill, accompanied by a faint hum. Outside the sun was high, and the leaves on the trees looked dusty, as though the weather was dry and hot. Then she remembered; the house was air-conditioned, like the ground floors of some of the big Tokyo department stores. How very strange!

Strange, too, were the deep-piled rug and the clutter of furniture and pictures. An inlaid-mahogany bureau, a nest of little tables, an armchair covered with green-and-white chintz to match the curtains at the windows, pictures on the painted walls, a door opening to a sparkling bathroom, which was, her grandmother had said, to be all her own!

Such luxury, a private bathroom! Quick as thought, Jenny Kimura slipped out of bed and ran across the floor in her bare feet, missing the cool smooth feel of *tatami*, but amused by the furry brush of the carpet. Like running her toes over Togo's back!

The bath was even more beautiful than she had remembered it from her first glimpse last night. The floor tiles were white flecked with gold, which sparkled in the sun. An oval washbowl was set into a long marble counter, above which a huge mirror reached to the ceiling and reflected a sparkling white tub and a row of green monogrammed towels. Jenny showered, then ran the tub full of warm water and lay in it, soaking in the traditional Japanese manner. Her grandmother, seeming to understand the weariness induced by excitement quite as much as the long hours in the air, had said she might sleep as late as she liked. A small clock on the bedside table announced that it was past ten, but Jenny felt no compulsion to hurry. She needed to renew her strength before she could face the many surprises bound to be in store for her today.

Besides, she wanted time to sort out the impressions, no matter how fleeting, that she had already received. The spaciousness of everything—the country, the city, even the house, which must be three times the size she might have imagined. One woman, living here alone!

One *old* woman, she almost thought, although her grandmother hadn't seemed especially old last night in her green dress. She had seemed tall and slender and energetic with her quick, long stride, her hair dusted with a silvery light, and her searching gray eyes. This morning, when Jenny went somewhat timidly downstairs and encountered her grandmother coming in from the terrace wearing Bermuda shorts, a sleeveless shirt, and gardening gloves, she seemed even less like a conventional grandmother.

"Hello, dear!" she called with quick gaiety. "I'm so glad you slept late. Never have I seen such a tired

54

child!" There was something about the use of the word *child* that disturbed Jenny. Or was it that the greeting was so casual—almost too casual, considering that she had just flown halfway across the world?

An orange-and-white cat, quite long-legged, with a proud, independent step and an intelligent face, appeared in the hall and rubbed his lean body along Mrs. Smith's bare legs.

"This is Freddy," Jenny's grandmother explained, as she bent to pick the animal up. "Freddy is a member of the family. He sleeps in the kitchen. That's why you didn't meet him last night."

"Hello, Freddy." Jenny moved forward to stroke the cat's head, but her grandmother was hurrying on.

"You must be hungry. Come, I'll give you some breakfast. Or Leona will, actually. Leona lives in, you know."

Leona proved to be black-skinned, plump, and kindly. She stopped polishing silver to gaze at Jenny with frank curiosity. "My land," she murmured. "My land, you *do* look Japanese."

Jenny laughed. "Do I? At home they say I look foreign."

Then she glanced at her grandmother and surprised a slight frown of annoyance, although her voice was controlled when she said, "Miss Jennifer would like some breakfast, Leona, when you have time."

"I have time right now, ma'am," Leona replied pleasantly, wiping her hands on her apron and approaching the refrigerator with a leisurely waddle. "I

55

saved you some orange juice, honey. And what else would you like? Eggs and bacon? Coffee or milk?"

"Just milk and toast, please," Jenny answered. Her stomach was still feeling a little queasy with excitement, and she glanced at her grandmother uneasily, wondering whether she should say straight out that everyone always called her Jenny Kimura—that Jennifer seemed outrageously fancy to her unaccustomed ear.

But she hesitated, and the opportunity was lost, because Leona began asking questions about whether she hadn't been scared on that great big jet airplane way up in the sky? "My goodness, you must be brave," she said. "Brave or foolish. I wouldn't go up in one on a bet, not me."

Meanwhile, Leona was moving from one point in the gleaming kitchen to another, while Jenny tried to conceal her fascination with her chocolate-colored skin and, instead, stared in admiration at the huge refrigerator, the stainless-steel ovens, the tabletop stove. She touched a formica counter lingeringly, and said, "This is so beautiful! It's just like the pictures in the magazines."

"It *is* a nice kitchen," her grandmother agreed. "I designed it myself. Men make fine architects, but they don't have much sense about kitchens, by and large."

Jenny smiled. "I can't wait to see the rest of the house," she admitted. "Will you take me on a tour?"

"Of course. Just as soon as you've had some breakfast. Come look me up on the terrace. I'm pruning some shrubs."

56

This corroborated Jenny's first impression that her grandmother was a person of great vigor. She was always doing something, but not at all the sort of things that Japanese women spent their days doing. She worked in the garden like a laborer and seemed to enjoy it, although she came back into the air-conditioned house with her hair tousled, her arms scratched, and her forehead beaded with perspiration. She acted as if it were the most natural thing in the world that a sixty-two-year-old woman should be dressed like a girl and working like a man.

"Now," she said, stripping off her gloves once more and swiping at her forehead with a handkerchief, "you want to see the house. It hasn't been changed much, except for the kitchen, since your father grew up here." A spasm of pain crossed her face and her jaw tightened. Is she feeling ill? Jenny wondered. Does she have arthritis, perhaps? But she was too polite to ask, and her grandmother turned and led her into the living room. "Most of the furniture is old," she said. "Philadelphia pieces that came down in my family." She stroked a tabletop. "I love the feel of waxed wood."

"Daddy said you had antiques. These are—antiques, then?"

Her grandmother nodded, but hurried on. "The dining room is just a dining room, like any other. Except for that painting over the sideboard, a Peale, and a rather good one, I think." Jenny contemplated the portrait of a gentleman in a stock and riding coat.

"An ancestor?" she asked.

Her grandmother nodded absently, and said, "You can wander around upstairs at any time. My bedroom is opposite yours. But now come and see the pool. It's just off the terrace, but a stone wall hides it from the kitchen wing."

"A pool?" Jenny envisioned a lotus pool, but this was a rectangular swimming pool that made her gasp with admiration. "Do you swim?" she asked in astonishment.

"Of course," said her grandmother, as though this were a very peculiar question. "I usually go in for a dip before breakfast. You must join me, any time you like."

"I'm sorry," said Jenny, feeling rather inadequate, "but I don't know how to swim."

"You don't know—?" Her grandmother swung around, obviously appalled. "Good heavens, child, what have you been doing all your life?"

Jenny gulped, but took the question seriously. "Living in Tokyo," she replied. "Going to school." She added, "Playing tennis sometimes."

Her grandmother seemed to recover. "You do play tennis then. Well, that's good. What about golf?"

It was Jenny who was now startled. She shook her head. "In Japan men play golf."

"Well, you must walk around with me someday," said her grandmother, a remark that Jenny didn't fully understand. But before she could question it the subject of swimming came up again. "I'll teach you," her grandmother promised. "You'll be paddling around like a fish inside of a week."

The directness and vigor of her grandmother's speech, it occurred to Jenny, matched the lean strength of her tanned hands. She was a spare woman, with an erect carriage, and her skin seemed to be surprisingly firm. Compared with Jenny's withered Japanese grandmother or with flabby Mrs. McAlpin, her airplane acquaintance, Mrs. Smith seemed almost young.

Only one thing struck Jenny as odd, a habit her grandmother had of quickly sliding her eyes away whenever their glances met. She would examine her granddaughter indirectly, sometimes with curiosity, but her eyes never lingered in affection, as the eyes of Jenny's parents did.

But of course we're strangers, really; it will take time to get to know one another, Jenny thought. And, after all, Americans are bound to be different. Daddy warned me that things might be awkward at first.

What exactly had he said? That his mother was a woman of high principles and strong prejudices. "Just be yourself and she'll grow to love you, but it may take a while."

Love was a word Jenny couldn't yet associate with her American grandmother, who seemed almost churlish in her acceptance of a strange young person in her house. Jenny felt as though she had been dropped down from outer space. She had expected all sorts of preliminaries—questions about her father, some mention at least of her mother, inquiries about her school. She had anticipated a gradual building up of an acquaintanceship, with the polite exchanges she was accustomed to and understood, but apparently all that was to be skipped. Jenny felt rather like a stray puppy who has been picked up on the street, who is fed and housed, but whose benefactor is indifferent to any need for affection and never takes time to cuddle or play.

This feeling persisted as the day wore on. Like a puppy, Jenny found herself trotting around at her grandmother's heels, trying to orient herself to this big, furniture-filled house and to find out what was expected of her. It was a distinct relief when Mrs. Smith announced after lunch that she must attend an important committee meeting, but would be back about five. She suggested that Jennifer either take a nap, read a book, or go lie by the pool in the sunshine. "When I get home I'll give you a swimming lesson," she said, then hurried off as though it was a relief to escape.

Actually, after her grandmother left, Jenny did none of these things. She wandered through the rooms, touching objects here and there, a chair arm, a figurine, the silver frame on a photograph of two earnest young boys—her father and his brother Richard? She gazed at the picture for some time, trying to imagine what they had been like, then went out to the kitchen in search of Leona.

"Excuse me," she said, coming to stand by the counter where a pie crust was being crimped, "but have you worked for my grandmother for a very long time?"

"It all depends what you call long," Leona drawled. " 'Bout five years, most likely."

This was disappointing. "Then you never met my father?"

"Land no, and to tell the Lord's honest truth, I never expected to meet you."

People in America keep saying the most incomprehensible things, Jenny thought with a sigh. How could she reply to a remark like that? Instead, she changed the subject. "Is there anything I can do to help?"

This seemed to amuse Leona. "Can you cook?" she asked.

Taking the question at face value, Jenny replied, "A little. My mother has taught me how to make *sukiyaki,* so that I can prepare it for my grandmother. She says that is the one Japanese dish all Americans seem to like."

Leona's forehead wrinkled in puzzlement. "Skaki? What's that?"

"Oh, it's delicious!" Jenny Kimura said, comforted to be on familiar ground. "It's a combination of beef and soy sauce and all sorts of sliced vegetables, cooked right at the table, in a chafing dish."

Leona looked relieved. "Well! Just so it isn't eel or one of them."

She went back to her pie making. "You like boysenberries?" she asked, as she tucked the finished creation into a shining oven.

"I've never tasted them," Jenny admitted. "Nor even heard of them, for that matter. But I love to try all sorts of new things."

"That's the way to talk," said Leona. "And you're

bound to have plenty of chances, pretty as you are. I bet you make a hit with the boys."

Jenny flushed, baffled by this unexpected shift in the conversation. "American girls think a lot about boys, don't they?"

"That's for sure," said Leona. "But is it any different where you come from?"

Jenny Kimura smiled. "Maybe not. Japanese girls dream about boys, but they don't really get to know any, at least not in high school. We see them in groups, of course, but we don't talk to any of them alone."

Leona turned in astonishment. "You're kidding?"

Jenny shook her head. "That *is* different then?"

Leona countered with another question. "You mean you've never had a boy friend?"

"Not really. You see I go to a girls' school."

Leona gave a long sigh, whether in consternation or anticipation Jenny couldn't guess. "You take it easy over here," she advised. "You just look 'em over, pleasantlike, but don't be too hasty in takin' your pick."

※ FIVE

Even though Leona's advice struck her as peculiar, the conversation was reassuring to Jenny. It was nice to be thought pretty, and it was exciting to look forward to meeting some young people. Subconsciously, it had troubled her that she might come into contact only with her grandmother's elderly friends.

Going up to her room, she sank down into the chintz-covered chair and took stock of the situation. One thing was certain; her grandmother was a continuing surprise. The dress she had worn to the committee meeting was bright yellow, an unthinkable color for any woman past middle age in Japan. Equally remarkable was the fact that Mrs. Smith drove a car, and that she apparently spent a great deal of time away from the house. She was a hospital Gray Lady—whatever that might be!—vice-president of her garden club, a member of a weekly bridge group, and a committee member for all sorts of charities.

Some of this information Jenny Kimura had gleaned from bits and pieces of overheard telephone calls. Indeed, the phone seemed to ring almost constantly during the late morning hours, and her grandmother kept turning the pages of an engagement book with one hand while she held the receiver in the other, making now a commitment, then an excuse. "My granddaughter has just arrived, you see."

"Don't worry about me," Jenny was impelled to say. "I'll be all right."

"Of course you will, dear," her grandmother had answered. "But I want to see you get acquainted first." Not "we" get acquainted? Shouldn't that be the first consideration?

Perhaps there were things that she should do, Jenny thought, gestures she must make. First of all, the presentation of gifts. She felt that this might be done most appropriately after the evening meal, so at dinner time, refreshed from the promised dip in the pool and the discovery that it was quite easy to stay afloat, she came downstairs bearing an armful of beautifully wrapped packages.

She put them on a chair in the entrance hall until after coffee was served, then presented them ceremoniously. "These are sent by my mother and father with deep affection and many thanks for your kindness to me." Then she knelt by her grandmother's chair and folded the discarded wrapping paper very neatly so that it could be used again, while Mrs. Smith exclaimed in delight at the beautiful Imari bowl, expressed surprise at the compactness of a pocket-size

64

transistor radio, admired the luster of the cultured pearls her son had chosen, and assured Jenny that it would be quite proper to give Leona one of the smaller mementos of Japan she had brought along. Jenny selected an oblong box containing a painted fan and took it out to the kitchen, then came back to find her grandmother staring in bemusement at the pearls she still held in her hands.

Jenny slipped quietly into a chair, thinking, Now she'll ask about my father, now we'll start getting acquainted. But instead her grandmother suddenly straightened her back and said with unexpected briskness, "I've asked some children over to meet you on Saturday night. For a cookout by the pool."

Was this her grandmother's return gift? Jenny wondered, uncertain of American customs. "That will be very nice," she said politely. "A cookout means hamburgers? I do like American hamburgers! Daddy sometimes makes them for Saturday lunch."

"Hamburgers and hot dogs," murmured Mrs. Smith absently, as she let the pearls trickle back into the little silk envelope in which they had arrived. Freddy came into the room and, seeing his mistress occupied, gave a soft miaow and leaped into Jenny's lap. She stroked him, smiling, and he started to purr, then turned in a full circle and settled down, arching his neck under her caress.

"I think he likes me," Jenny said, and suddenly there was a lump in her throat and she felt very, very far away from home and Togo, from school and Yukari, but most of all from her parents and the familiar simplicity of the house in which she had been raised.

Trying to conquer the emotion, she sat looking down at the cat, her hair falling forward over her shoulders, pride coming too slowly to her aid. What was her grandmother saying? That there would be perhaps a dozen guests, most of them from this same section of town, girls who went to Sunset and Barstow, boys who went to Pembroke Country Day.

Jenny nodded and managed to look up, as soon as she felt that her courage was restored. "Japanese are very much interested in American young people," she said.

The remark was intended to be courteous, and she was thinking of Yukari quite as much as she was thinking of herself, but for some reason her grandmother seemed indignant. "Remember, Jennifer, that you are only *partly* Japanese," Mrs. Smith admonished her, and the fact that she smiled when she spoke did not make her voice less sharp. Then, in the next breath, she tried to apologize. "Of course, I realize that, being raised abroad, you've picked up a lot of Oriental ideas, but I think it's time now to cultivate your American heritage, don't you?"

"I guess so," Jenny murmured, not quite sure what her grandmother meant.

"It may be difficult at first, but you'll get acclimated," Mrs. Smith continued cheerfully.

Jenny nodded. "I'll try very hard," she promised. Then she added seriously, "You must help me. You must please tell me when I do things wrong."

"You won't do things wrong," her grandmother replied, quite sincerely. "You have beautiful manners, my dear, and that's more than I can say for some of your contemporaries. You'll see!"

Nevertheless, as the night of the party approached, Jenny felt more and more apprehensive. In the interim she had been introduced to some of the physical aspects of Kansas City, the downtown business section, the Mission Hills suburb where her grandmother lived, and the Plaza District's beautiful shops, housed behind Spanish façades. She had gone driving through miles and miles of winding roads lined with handsome houses, roads twisting along brooks and beside golf courses, until suddenly the trees became mere saplings, and strips of macadam with unfinished houses on either side led straight out into country fields. A sense of space pervaded everything. Big stores, big houses, big boulevards, big cars in which to travel around this huge country that defied the imagination. Jenny was enthralled, even though she felt strange and uncertain of herself.

On the day of the cookout she paid her first visit to a supermarket, where she pushed a cart around for her grandmother and stared, big-eyed, at a greater variety of foods than she had ever before seen. Quickly, almost haphazardly, Mrs. Smith picked up packages and boxes and cans, hurrying from one aisle to another with complete familiarity. "There," she said, when the cart was piled high with groceries, "I think that ought to do."

As Jenny, still in charge of the cart, waited her

turn at a check-out counter, Mrs. Smith went off to pick up one last purchase and came back with a friend in tow. This large, smiling woman rushed up to Jenny in a manner that was almost too cordial. "My dear!" she cried, holding out her hands. "Your grandmother's been hiding you from all of us." Then she turned to Jenny's grandmother. "Oh, Jennifer, isn't she just like a big doll!"

Jenny blushed furiously. She couldn't help it. Accustomed to restraint in dealing with strangers, she found such ebullience embarrassing. Yet she could see that the woman meant no harm, and when her grandmother introduced Mrs. Marshall, she shook hands politely and answered her questions with the expected smile.

"We're shopping for a cookout," Mrs. Smith said gaily, as though she wanted to keep the conversation general. "Far from hiding my granddaughter, Emily, I've asked a dozen young people in to meet her tonight!"

"Well, that's as it should be," said Mrs. Marshall, but without removing her appraising gaze from Jenny's face. She added, with a twinkle in her eyes, "You'll be quite a novelty."

"Do I seem so *very* different?" Jenny asked artlessly when she and her grandmother had transferred the packages from the cart to the car and were once more alone.

"Well, yes, you do," Mrs. Smith confessed unequivocally. "Not that it's necessarily a handicap." She hesitated a moment, then said, "Jennifer, my dear, you must expect to be looked over with a certain curiosity by my friends. After all, they've been speculating for years on what the child of a mixed marriage might be like."

"Mixed marriage?" Jenny murmured. "You mean my mother and my father?"

"Of course, dear. There's no use mincing words."

"I knew you disapproved," said Jenny, her voice dropping to a mere whisper. "I knew you were shocked, because your other son was killed in the war—"

Her grandmother didn't speak, so Jenny stumbled on. "But I—I didn't—" Then she came to a dead halt, and in a completely different tone of voice said, after a few seconds, "Grandmother, I wish you'd call me Jenny, or Jenny Kimura, the way everybody else does. It's a very pretty name, of course, but I don't feel like a Jennifer."

Afterward she was sorry, because the outburst had been rude and her grandmother had looked quite abashed. Jenny tried, by being especially helpful, to erase the memory of the painful conversation. She carried the heavy bags of groceries to Leona in the kitchen, lugged charcoal to the outdoor grill, helped set up the supper table with the necessary picnic equipment, and, only when everything was in order, slipped away to her room to bathe and change.

She showered, then soaked, Japanese fashion, in a full tub of clean water, and reappraised the situation. She had been blind, utterly blind! Long before this she should have perceived that her grandmother was ashamed of her! Then why had the invitation to visit been extended, and why had Daddy allowed her to accept? When he must have realized—he must have known!

Of course he had known! Jenny could recall the concern in his eyes when he'd said, "It may take a while . . . just be yourself."

Yet she felt betrayed. By her father, who expected so much of her. By her grandmother, whose heartiness too lightly cloaked a deep resentment from which she had never recovered. How could she—Jenny—one young stranger in a strange land—hope to joust in such an unequal tournament?

She wished she could call on some magic to whisk her straight back home where she was loved and cherished. Only Leona, whose curiosity had been frank and disarming, was settling into a wholehearted acceptance. Jenny quaked as she imagined the evening. Eleven young Americans to whom she was likely to appear only a Japanese doll.

There was a knock at her door. "I'm going downstairs, dear. Come along when you're ready!"

"Five minutes," Jenny called back, and reluctantly got out of the tub.

She didn't look in the mirror as she dressed, and she didn't choose her costume with any special care. She felt dead inside, unready to make any effort, and yet she knew that a truly valiant effort was necessary. As the guest of honor she must be prepared to exert every possible charm.

Her father would expect it of her. At this thought

Jenny's head came up with a jerk. He hadn't betrayed her, really. He'd tried to forewarn her. And he'd said, quite clearly, that it wouldn't be easy. She couldn't be a quitter; she'd just have to do her best.

So it was with outward poise, the smooth, impenetrable good manners she had learned from her mother, that Jenny greeted the first of the guests, two boys in shorts and open-necked shirts who were big, blond, handsome, and, by Japanese standards, rather gauche. They were the Abell twins, Nick and Jerry, and were followed by a trio of two girls and another boy, this one thin and studious-looking, with an uncropped head of bristling dark hair. "John Sears," said Mrs. Smith, presenting him. "The grandson of a very dear friend of mine."

John held out a limp hand, and seemed startled by Jenny's remarkably strong grip. "Hi, there," he said, then, seeming in doubt as to how to proceed, wandered away.

Turning back to the girls, Jenny was awe-struck by their long-limbed beauty. One was a tall, creamy-skinned redhead, who looked like a fashion model for *Seventeen,* and the other was as small-boned as Jenny Kimura herself, with a neat size-six figure and a warm smile. "What fun to have you here!" she exclaimed ingenuously. "I can't wait to ask you all sorts of questions about Japan!"

More young people were introduced, and moved on to pick up bottles of Coke or ginger ale from the refreshment table. Only the Abell boys, who Jenny correctly assumed must be college freshmen, chose beer. Last to arrive were a brother and sister named Alan and Janet Carlisle, who came in breathlessly and apologetically, explaining that they'd had a flat tire.

"No wonder, that old jalopy you kids drive!" called Nick Abell. "Why don't you get a good car like mine?"

"Yours?" scoffed Alan, not in the least offended. "Yours is one of these late-model deals. Mine has character!" He turned to Jenny. "Want a new experience? After supper I'll take you for a ride in my 1925 Ford."

"I'd like that!" Jenny said at once, her eyes sparkling. This lighthearted lad appealed to her. He had a pleasant Kansas drawl, a quick smile, and a bouncy manner of walking, which reminded her of her father's gait.

Meanwhile, commandeered by Mrs. Smith, the Abell twins had lighted a charcoal fire. Several of the group had changed to bathing suits and were splashing around the pool, but the Carlisles refused an invitation to swim on the basis that they had arrived too late. Instead, Janet allowed Jenny to get her a soft drink while Alan joined Nick and continued the good-natured argument over the merits of their respective cars. Watching him out of the corner of her eye, Jenny thought he must be typically American, easygoing and uncomplicated. He was the type she and Yukari had envisioned when they tried to imagine what Occidental boys would be like.

"I've been dying to meet you," Janet said frankly, when she accepted the drink Jenny brought her. "So has Alan. We had a Japanese girl at our school last year, but I didn't get to know her very well, probably because she had trouble with English." She added, "You speak with no accent at all."

Jenny smiled. "Remember, my father is American."

"But do you speak Japanese just as well?"

"Of course."

"Aren't you lucky!" Janet cried. "I know only one other girl our age who is truly bilingual, and she lived for years and years in Paris. When I go to college I want to get really solid in a foreign language, but I have a feeling it will have to be something relatively easy like Spanish or French."

"Stop talking serious talk," adjured the willowy redhead, coming up the pool steps and shaking her hair like a spaniel. "What I want to know about is *geishas*. Are they really as exotic and mysterious as they look in magazines?"

Jenny laughed spontaneously. "I wouldn't be a judge," she admitted. "I've only seen them in pictures myself."

This seemed to amuse Janet, as did the disappointed expression on her companion's face. "Lorna has a notion they grow up all over the place, like dandelions or Hollywood starlets. But as a matter of fact, how many movie actresses have *we* ever seen except on the screen?"

Interrupting this discussion, Alan appeared to ask the girls how they liked their hamburgers, medium or rare?

"Rare, please," replied Lorna at once, and Janet nodded.

In her turn Jenny said, "Well done, if possible," a remark from which Alan recoiled in pretended horror. Gently, almost apologetically, she admitted, "I don't think I'll ever grow to like rare meat."

"That's O.K.," said the boy with a grin that excused her. "You can have it any way you like."

After this encounter, for a reason she couldn't define, Jenny stopped worrying about being accepted. The party ceased being a strain, and she was able to move from group to group and make conversation without feeling especially awkward or shy. They still treated her like a duckling who had mistakenly wandered into a brood of swans, but she didn't mind it. She was both interested in and curious about these young Americans, and she showed it, but in such a manner that they found it entertaining to show off for a stranger in their midst.

Inevitably, Jenny liked some of the group better than others, but only a soft, plump girl named Ada Parsons did she find difficult. Ada, she realized almost at once, was the only one of the entire lot who regarded her—as she had feared and dreaded—not as a person but as a doll.

It was a subtle distinction, but Jenny wasn't just imagining it. There was a sidelong manner in which Ada glanced at her, and a too-cheery manner of speaking. "Goodness, but you have a nice tan! Or is that the real color of your skin?"

"It's the real color," Jenny said, realizing that while

74

in Tokyo she appeared fair, here she looked as though she had spent many days in the sun.

"Oh," said Ada, halting abruptly as though she had made a social gaffe. She looked away, then back to Jenny, but without meeting her eyes. "Well, you're lucky, aren't you, not to have to *work* for a tan? I burn just horribly myself!"

There was nothing Jenny could put her finger on, but something was vaguely wrong with everything Ada said. Either she dislikes me or I frighten her, Jenny thought, but she couldn't quite decide between the two possibilities.

John Sears came over with a long fork in his hand and invited her to cook her own hot dog, an invitation Jenny readily accepted. Food was disappearing with a rapidity that astonished her. There was none of the formality to which she was accustomed in Japan. Indeed, the most surprising things took place. Lorna and Nick, both in bathing suits, began to play at the pool's edge like a couple of puppies, fell in, and came up laughing, only to try to duck one another in spluttering glee.

"Hey, quit splashing!" somebody called, but they paid no attention.

Janet, seeing Jenny's puzzled expression, seemed to understand. "We're not noted for politeness," she murmured, "but it's all in good clean fun."

Once the party was launched, Mrs. Smith stayed in the background, sending Leona out to the terrace with dessert—two fresh strawberry pies, heaped high with whipped cream. They disappeared as fast as the rest of the food, although Jenny refused her portion. "It looks delicious, but I just can't," she said with a sigh.

Inside the house, Mrs. Smith started the record player, which she had stacked with popular music early in the afternoon, and a couple or two started dancing in a desultory fashion, their faces expressionless, their eyes half closed. Jenny stood in the shadow of the wall and watched them in fascination, until Alan came up and said, "Still want to go for a ride?"

"Oh yes! But will it be all right?"

"For fifteen minutes? Sure!"

He held out his hand, but Jenny shyly backed away. In Japan nobody had ever tried to touch her, and she felt uneasy and uncertain of herself. Was this a custom here, like pairing off at suppertime and ignoring the common courtesies?

Suddenly Alan burst out laughing. "What are you afraid of? I won't bite."

But Jenny put her hands behind her back, although she smiled mischievously. Then suddenly she ran on ahead.

This seemed to amuse him even more, but he didn't persist, just kept chuckling as he followed her up the garden steps and around to the drive, where a boxlike automobile, set high on its axles, stood like an outsized toy beside the late-model cars. Opening the door, Alan allowed Jenny to climb into the front seat by herself. "It's a real tin lizzie," he said, "and, as such, is a collector's item hereabouts." He started the rackety engine and shouted above the roar, "I got it dirt cheap, then took it apart and put it together again myself!"

The pride in his voice made Jenny say, "Really?" in admiration.

"Yep. It was fun—and good experience."

With every remark Alan made, Jenny found herself liking him better. There was so much vigor about him, such enthusiasm.

"See the side curtains. Aren't they neat?"

"Neat?" Jenny questioned, because the outmoded shades were both ragged and soiled.

"An expression we have. American slang. Boy, you've got a lot to learn!"

"I'm beginning to realize that," Jenny confessed. Every now and then this evening some scrap of conversation had been completely unintelligible.

"Not nearly as much, though, as I'd have to learn if I should get plunked down in Japan."

Jenny tried to picture the prospect. "If the weather were as hot as this," she told him, "you'd be carrying a fan."

"A fan? *Me?*" Alan sounded horrified.

"Of course," said Jenny amiably. "Almost all men and boys carry fans in Japan, even though they wear kimonos only very occasionally."

Braking as he came to a crossroad, Alan shook his head. Then he leaned forward, listening to the snorting engine. "Hear that purr!" he murmured, dropping the subject in favor of his first love, the Ford.

Jenny allowed herself to be impressed as she jounced along on the high seat, which rested on broken springs. "Want to drive her?" Alan asked unexpectedly. "I can teach you the gearshift in a sec."

Jenny didn't admit that she couldn't drive. Instead she said, "I'm sixteen and I don't have a license."

Alan accepted this casually. "I'll show you how the gears work anyway. They're so old-fashioned they're kind of fun."

Although she listened with apparent attention, Jenny learned very little, because her mind kept drifting away from the gears to the boy at her side. She was intensely curious about him, for he was the very first boy with whom she had spent even a few minutes quite alone. Wouldn't Yukari be envious! This was what they had dreamed of, a chance to get to know what boys were really like!

Alan interested her, Jenny told herself, because he was a *typical* American, not because he had attractive blue-gray eyes and chestnut hair. But when she glanced at him surreptitiously her heart raced. If only she knew how to intrigue him. "Be yourself," her mother had said on parting, but Jenny thought that at this particular moment she'd rather be Lorna, who looked so sophisticated and glamorous.

"You're not listening!" scolded Alan suddenly, and turned the car back toward home. Jenny's heart fell, but she didn't protest. The adventure was over. And, to be sure, it was high time she returned to her guests.

Pulling into the drive, Alan yanked at the creaking hand brake and switched off the high-set headlights. "How about going to a drive-in tomorrow night?" he asked so unexpectedly that Jenny's fingers on the door handle tightened convulsively.

"A drive-in? You mean a—a movie?"

"That's right."

"With you—alone?" Jenny was grateful that the darkness hid the fact that she was trembling.

Alan laughed. "I told you I won't bite."

Jenny flushed and bit her lip, ashamed of her inexperience. "I'd love to!" she wanted to cry, but obeying her Japanese training rather than her own instinct, she replied, with beguiling primness, "I'll have to ask my grandmother."

✿ SIX

Jenny drifted through the rest of the evening in a dream. An American boy had asked her for a date, a boy named Alan Carlisle, who was tall and strong and deep-voiced, almost a man really. She could hardly wait to write to Yukari! In the very first week she had been here an American boy had asked her for a date!

It made her feel included, in a very special sort of way. Alan had said, "I'll phone you in the morning," so she wasn't faced with the necessity of approaching her grandmother immediately. She could hold the wonderful knowledge close and cherish it as a secret for a while.

Alan liked her! He must like her or he wouldn't have asked her, right away like that, to go out alone. It made Jenny feel infinitely superior, inches taller. What a perfectly marvelous thing to have happened to her!

It didn't matter that she saw little of Alan for the next hour or so. He was there, somewhere, among the couples who moved in and out of the circle of light. From Jenny's point of view it had turned into a rather peculiar party, with no games, no group singing. Boys and girls paired off quite independently, some of them dancing, others sitting on the edge of the pool, but all of them acting as though they owed no obligation to the hostess or to anyone else.

It was a relief, actually, when the last of the guests finally said good-night and the terrace was deserted. Jenny helped pick up the empty bottles and crumpled paper napkins, but her eyes were heavy with fatigue. It had been a long evening, albeit an exciting one. Her mind was still filled with thoughts of Alan—the way his hands looked on the wheel of the car, the timbre of his deep, laughing voice, the sparkle of curiosity in his eyes. Would this be a good time to ask her grandmother's permission to go out with him?

But as shyness made her hesitate, Jenny became aware that her grandmother was saying, "I think they enjoyed themselves. Otherwise, they wouldn't have stayed so late."

Jenny nodded. "They were nice. Very kind to me."

"Why shouldn't they be?" Mrs. Smith sounded edgy, perhaps from weariness. Then, as Jenny tried to frame a soothing answer, a strange sound came out of the blackness beyond the terrace lights.

"What's that?"

Turning in instinctive alarm, the pair stared into

81

the dark, listening anxiously. "It sounds like Freddy," Jenny said, as the cry came again. "Could he be hurt?"

"Oh, I hope not!" Mrs. Smith started forward, then stopped short as the cat appeared at the edge of the half-moon of light. He was holding his head high, carrying something in his mouth, and the strange, high-pitched mewling noise announced his coming. He sounded proud, as though he were bringing a trophy to his mistress, who shrank back in distaste. "Good heavens, child, I think he's got a mouse!"

Jenny thought so too. In fact, she was almost sure of it. But the mouse must be quite dead, because the object in Freddy's mouth did not move. "What do you want me to do?" she asked with more courage than she felt. "Take it away from him?"

"Oh, could you? Would you?" In a split second Mrs. Smith had turned into a cringing Victorian gentlewoman, unconsciously wringing her hands.

Meanwhile, Freddy was stalking deliberately forward, determined to lay his prize at his owner's feet. Never had Jenny seen an animal so filled with self-esteem. He had the dignity of a tiger bringing in his kill.

"Ugh!" Mrs. Smith put a chair between herself and her pet; then suddenly both she and Jenny saw what Freddy was carrying. It wasn't a dead mouse at all! It was a half-eaten hot dog.

They burst out laughing simultaneously. There was something so ludicrous about Freddy's pride in his capture that they almost collapsed with amusement, tired as they both were. "Oh, Jenny!" Mrs. Smith gasped. "Oh, Jenny, isn't he ridiculous!"

Not Jennifer—Jenny! She had used the nickname spontaneously for the first time. And in her merriment she seemed not even aware of her concession. Jenny's heart leaped with hope. Maybe Daddy was right after all! Maybe she and her grandmother could someday be friends.

Jenny instinctively reached out for love. She needed to be liked; she needed to be cosseted and warmed by affection. Only then could she feel secure and safe. So, anxious not to disturb this first feeling of rapport with her American grandmother, she put off the question of Alan's invitation until morning, even though it might take more courage to broach the subject in the cold light of day.

But, surprisingly, Mrs. Smith didn't seem to consider the idea of going to the movies with a boy—a boy *alone*—at all odd. Nor did Jenny admit that in Tokyo no boy would have dared ask her, not while she was still in high school. Dating of this sort was for the college crowd.

"Of course you may go," her grandmother said. "Alan Carlisle's a nice boy."

More than nice, Jenny wanted to shout. He's romantic and exciting and wonderful! But she put all this into a letter to Yukari instead, then spent the rest of the day washing her hair and trying to decide what to wear.

Finally she settled on the pink cotton. The full skirt would be comfortable for sitting, and she could

83

wear a matching band to hold her dark hair back from her ears. Oh, she wanted to look lovely—lovely! —tonight.

Yet, when Leona called up the stairs, "Miss Jenny, there's a young man here waitin' for you!" Jenny took a last look in the mirror and was vaguely dissatisfied by her appearance. Her hair was so very black and straight, her eyes so tilted. Trying to gather self-confidence, she reminded herself that Yukari and the other girls at school considered her light-skinned and American. But here she looked very Japanese.

How foolish you are to care! Alan *likes* you, Jenny scolded herself as she ran down to the entrance hall. Alan grinned and said, "Hi, there!" in a way that was half-amused, half-admiring. Mrs. Smith, who was writing checks in her study, looked up and called, "Have fun, children. Don't be late," then returned to her work.

So very different, Jenny thought, from the procedure at home, where any guest would have been greeted with bows, offered a welcoming cup of tea, and expected to pay his polite respects to the family. But then everything in the United States moved at an accelerated pace, including the business of getting acquainted with a boy. Alan was as easy as though they had known one another since childhood. As his car snorted and coughed its way down the drive, he glanced at Jenny winningly. "So you've never been to a passion pit before?"

"A *what?*" Jenny couldn't believe her ears.

84

"That's what we call a drive-in," explained Alan with a chuckle. "Slang again."

"Oh." Jenny breathed a sigh of relief.

"It's not too far wrong," offered Alan conversationally. "Lots of kids go there to make out."

Again Jenny was baffled, but she didn't pursue the subject. Instead, she said what was uppermost in her mind. "Excuse me if I am very excited. I have never before had a real date with a boy."

"You're kidding!"

Jenny shook her head. "In Japan, at our age, we only do things in groups."

"Our age?" Alan scoffed. "I'm years older than you. I was eighteen last month, and I'll be going to Williams in the fall."

"Williams—is that a college?"

"One of the best!"

"Aren't you fortunate!" breathed Jenny. "In Japan boys seventeen and eighteen study very hard to prepare for college. It is very difficult to get into a good school."

"Don't think it isn't here!"

"Oh, I'm sure you must be very clever," Jenny said admiringly, "but at least here there are many universities and colleges. In Japan there are very few."

"Tell me more about Japanese students," urged Alan when she paused. "What do they train for? What do they want to be?"

Jenny shrugged. "Only the lucky ones know. But everyone is sure that the big, prosperous companies will only employ bright students from first-class universities, so the competition is terrible."

"What happens if they flunk the entrance exams?"

"They become *ronin*," Jenny said sadly.

"*Ronin?*"

How could she explain? "Yes, it is an old word used during the Edo period of our history. Back in the seventeenth century most *samurai*—warriors—belonged to a master who paid them a stipend. *Ronin* were *samurai* who didn't have masters, just as these students don't have a university. Do you see?"

"Vaguely," said Alan. "Vaguely. Why don't these kids go to work?"

"Oh, nobody can get a good job unless he finishes school," replied Jenny instantly. "We are under the protection of our parents, just as you are."

"Just as I am! Hmph!" snorted Alan. "I've worked every summer since I was in the eighth grade!"

"But why?" cried Jenny in astonishment. "You're rich. You have your own car!"

"I bought it myself," said Alan proudly, "and it only cost a hundred bucks."

"But even so—"

"Oh, well," Alan said, disparaging his own bragging. "In the U.S. most kids work during summer vacation. It's supposed to teach us the value of money or something. Responsibility, I guess."

"Are you working this summer?" asked Jenny admiringly.

"Sure."

"Where?" Jenny probed.

86

"In a gas station. It's better than cutting lawns for a gardening crew. I did that last year."

Jenny couldn't visualize Alan at a gas-station job, because the environment wasn't familiar to her, but she could see him swinging along behind a mower, tall and strong on his long, straight legs, stripped to the waist in the heat of the day, glowing with a healthy suntan. Next to the slight Japanese boys she knew, and whom she never saw in any costume but a school uniform—white shirt, black trousers, and high-necked brass-buttoned jacket—Alan seemed as robust as the American hero of a cowboy-and-Indian film.

They had zigzagged cross-country until they were far out in the suburbs, running along a boulevard that led straight along the state line. Dusk was turning to darkness when Alan turned off the road, stopped at a booth where he handed two bills to a ticket seller, and rolled the car into position in front of a giant screen, set right out in the middle of a mowed field.

Hundreds of cars had already gathered, each parked beside a post containing individual loudspeaker equipment, but it was the size of the screen that fascinated Jenny. "Goodness!" she breathed. "It's enormous! And look at the number of cars!"

"Don't you have drive-ins in Japan?"

"Oh no," said Jenny promptly. "There isn't room."

"Not even in the country?"

"Well—maybe very far out. But most Japanese don't have cars, you see. We travel on subways or buses." Unconsciously Jenny was aligning herself with her mother's countrymen. "No, we have many, many things marked *Made in U.S.*, but drive-ins we can never have."

With darkness the program commenced, but until the feature appeared Alan felt there was no need to stop talking. Jenny, meanwhile, kept an eye on the passing scene. Whole families came and went from their cars to a refreshment booth, bearing ice-cream cones, hot dogs, popsicles, or hamburgers, depending on their appetite or inclination. It was like a continual mobile picnic, and it seemed that very few had come to watch the giants moving about on the wide screen. But with the beginning of the feature there was less activity. The rows of cars looked like ranks of dominoes, and only the bright pinpoints of cigarette tips occasionally punctured the darkness.

Jenny settled back on the seat, adjusting herself to the thrust of the broken springs. Then she tried to concentrate on the motion picture, which was set in the Deep South. The characters spoke with an accent she had never before heard, as different from a Kansas City drawl as Hokkaido Japanese was from the speech of Tokyo.

In spite of herself, however, her thoughts kept slipping away. She was thrillingly aware of Alan's nearness, of the pleasant scrubbed smell of his skin, of the way his hair grew untidily down the back of his neck, of the clean-cut line of his jaw, glimpsed in profile by the headlights of a late-arriving car. Yet she was relieved that Alan didn't put his arm around her, as she had seen a boy in the next lane do, embracing the fair-haired girl he was with as though they were quite alone. Although Jenny wanted very much to learn the manners of her father's country, she was shocked by this behavior. In Japan such freedom was only permitted a couple engaged to be married —and then they were careful of their manners in a public place!

Her companion, however, seemed interested only in the unfolding of the screen romance, and finally Jenny became accustomed to the accent and better able to understand. Indeed, the end came too soon. She sighed and shifted position while Alan stretched and yawned. "Had enough?" he asked.

"Enough? Isn't it over?"

"It's a double feature," Alan explained patiently, "but we don't have to stay."

"Grandmother," Jenny remembered, "said not to be late."

"O.K. Let's go." Alan started the rackety engine and snaked through the rows of parked cars toward the gate, while Jenny tried to imagine what would happen when the second film was over. Would the cars depart smoothly, one by one, or would these impetuous Americans get into a hopeless snarl, trying to beat one another to the exits?

She was about to consult Alan, when he said, "I'm starved. Let's stop for something to eat." A few minutes later he led her through the door of a brightly lighted coffee shop, set in a macadam parking area right in the middle of a field.

Once more Jenny was thrust into a totally new environment, dominated by noise. Dishes were clat-

tering, a jukebox was playing, and dozens of people
—young and old—were eating and laughing and talking, even though the hour was approaching midnight.
Alan led Jenny to an empty booth, where they consulted large printed menus. "What would you like?
A hamburger?"

"I'm not very hungry," Jenny murmured, finding the
menu complicated and confusing. Then she brightened. "I know. Chocolate ice cream and a doughnut.
Is that all right?"

Alan looked amused, but said, "Of course," and
repeated the order to a withered, white-haired waitress
in a starched pink uniform.

Caught staring at the woman, Jenny flushed. "I'm
sorry," she apologized, "but isn't it sad that an old
woman must work so hard!"

"Don't women work in Japan?"

"Yes, but in the house mostly. Japanese waitresses
are all very young girls who have left school and are
waiting to get married. Nobody would employ an
old woman like that."

Alan looked puzzled. "But she probably *needs* the
work."

"Where is her family? Her children?" Jenny wished
the conversation hadn't taken this turn, but she couldn't
help being distressed.

Shrugging, Alan replied, "Lots of older women work,
if their husbands die or if their children are grown up
and gone." The orders came and he broke off, then
began to spoon sauces on his hamburger while Jenny

attacked her sugar-coated cruller very daintily with a fork.

Alan watched her for a moment, then burst out laughing.

"What's wrong?" Jenny questioned soberly. "Not very proper?" She put the fork down on her plate in embarrassment.

"Too proper!" Alan teased. "You just pick up a doughnut in your fingers, like a piece of bread."

While Jenny experimented he sat back and continued to look at her with amusement. She met his eyes, then glanced down at her plate, afraid that she might betray how much she wanted his approval.

As though he sensed her desire, he leaned forward and said gently, "You're an easy girl to be with, Jenny. Gentle, sort of. And I like the way you talk."

Such flattery was so sweet and unexpected that Jenny felt quite nonplussed. "I like the way you talk, too," she murmured just above a whisper. "Oh, it's been a wonderful evening, Alan. I'm having such a good time."

"But it's been too short," Alan complained with a sudden frown. "What about tomorrow? Invite me for a swim after I finish work. I won't say no."

❀ SEVEN

For the next fortnight Jenny saw Alan Carlisle almost every day. He finished up at the gas station about four o'clock, and as the weather became increasingly hot and humid he made a habit of dropping in for a dip before dinner.

Mrs. Smith gladly turned over to him the job of teaching Jenny to swim, and within the first week he taught her to do a fairly presentable crawl. A few days later she was timidly diving off the side of the pool, and by the end of two weeks she was practicing a simple front dive from the board.

"Great!" Alan cried, the first time she managed to avoid doing a belly flop. "I'll make an athlete of you yet!" And Jenny, willing to try anything he asked, was certain that she was the luckiest girl in the world.

Meanwhile, life in the Smith household had settled into a sort of routine. Jenny grew accustomed to the fact that her grandmother hurried to and fro on errands throughout the day, and when she felt the need of companionship she turned to Leona in the kitchen.

Leona teased her about Alan at every opportunity. "The cream of the crop," she called him. "My, I bet the other girls are jealous of you!"

Jenny could have told her that the interest of the "other girls" in her affairs was negligible. Lorna had invited her, with a few other friends, to a duty lunch, but all of this group had chattered among themselves, obviously finding Jenny uncomfortably foreign and difficult to talk to. Janet Carlisle had made the most effort, setting up a game of doubles at the country-club tennis courts, and introducing Jenny to some of the crowd there. But even she seemed utterly involved in her own life, making room to include Jenny, but not deeply concerned.

It didn't matter. Nothing really mattered but Alan. Jenny lived for the next time she would see him. In the interim she went through the motions of being a dutiful guest. She helped her grandmother arrange flowers, carried her bags when they went shopping, and even trudged around the golf course with her in the hot morning sun.

"This is a good game for a woman my age," Mrs. Smith said one day, as they walked from the clubhouse to the first tee. "Keeps up my muscle tone. Though I must say my score isn't what it used to be."

"I think you play very well, Grandmother," Jenny said.

Mrs. Smith chuckled. "You sound like Red Riding Hood," she accused, "and I expect sometimes I act

93

like the wolf." But then she became unexpectedly confidential. "You know," she said, "there were years and years when I didn't play golf at all. When I started to shoot in the 90's I just gave it up."

"Why?" Jenny asked curiously.

"I began to beat my own husband," Mrs. Smith admitted ruefully. "He didn't like it a bit. It hurt his ego. On the other hand, he didn't enjoy playing with a dub, so I was between the devil and the deep blue sea. Actually, Jenny, you may be wise to resist the game. There's no place for a woman golfer who wants to play with other than her own sex."

Remarks like this Jenny remembered and repeated in letters to her parents, as especially descriptive of her grandmother, whom she still found surprising and occasionally formidable. There continued to be only fleeting moments of sympathy between them. "I haven't got to know her very well yet, but she is kind—" Jenny hesitated, then added, "—and happy to have me here."

Happy, however, wasn't quite the word for it. Her grandmother didn't really seem happy. She seemed strained sometimes. As though I am a duty or a responsibility she has decided to assume, thought Jenny, and as though she is almost afraid of me. The emotion Jenny could sense was too complex to understand, but it was apparent that her grandmother was a cheerful woman, although not a happy one.

Searching for the cause, Jenny reminded herself that her grandmother was a widow; this might account for everything. She was anxious to ask a great many questions about her late grandfather, but solicitude restrained her. She had a young person's belief that the elderly are reluctant to discuss the dead.

It was Alan who drove her, one Sunday afternoon, down through the deserted business section of the city, to the stockyard district and along the river, to see the grain elevator once owned by Smith and Colby, her grandfather's brokerage firm. "It isn't the largest—that's owned by Santa Fe and has a ten-million-bushel capacity—but it's still a big one," said Alan admiringly, as he stopped the car at a vantage point from which they could see the full height of the structure. He explained how the automatic car dumpers worked, and how the grain was cleaned and conditioned and graded before it was shipped to various parts of the world.

Jenny was impressed. "My grandfather must have been a very important man in Kansas City."

"I guess he was," Alan said, as though he'd never given the subject much thought. Then he grinned. "After all, your grandmother is very comfortable."

"You mean she's rich?"

"Well, not everybody has a big house like that, and a maid and a swimming pool."

This would certainly have held true in Tokyo, but in America how could one judge? Most of Mrs. Smith's friends seemed equally well-to-do, considering the way in which they lived. But then Jenny had seen no poor people at all—at least, not poor by Japanese standards. The American Midwest seemed a land of

95

plenty, and these terminals for cattle and grains only confirmed the impression.

Her thoughts returned to her grandfather, whom a photograph depicted as a ruddy, husky man with a shock of pure-white hair. She tried to imagine him, coming downtown every day, buying and selling wheat, rye, corn, and barley, dealing in futures, a sort of gambling operation Alan had tried unsuccessfully to explain. She felt that this sort of man must epitomize the Midwest. It was not, after all, a land of cowboys and Indians, as she had once supposed. It was a thriving region, built by businessmen like her grandfather, and this made her feel proud.

"What are you going to do when you get out of school?" Jenny asked Alan unexpectedly.

"I don't know," he replied, frowning. "I wish I did. It worries me."

"Would you like to be a grain merchant?"

Alan hooted. "Not me! I have no head for figures, or for bargaining."

"What does your father do?"

"He's a banker," Alan said, "a trust officer. He deals with investments and things."

"My father's a banker too," Jenny Kimura said, considering it a coincidence. "I don't think he likes it much, though. He'd rather be working with his bonsai."

"His what?" Alan was fascinated by any unfamiliar Japanese references.

"Bonsai," Jenny repeated. "They're miniature trees, grown in shallow pots. Some of them are very beautiful and very old. They say the Emperor has several pines that have been in pots for five hundred years!"

She told Alan all she knew about the raising of the little trees—how the roots must be clipped, the branches pruned, the trunks trained with wire—and he listened attentively. Then, as they drove back to the suburbs, he said, "You know, I've found out why I like to be with you, Jenny. You talk about *things.*"

Jenny wasn't sure that this was praise. "Not very feminine?" she inquired.

Instead of listening to her, Alan was looking at her. "Very feminine," he replied with emphasis.

When they reached the house Mrs. Smith was making sandwiches for Sunday-night supper, since Leona was off for the day. She invited Alan to stay, and he accepted with alacrity, telephoning his mother to say that he wouldn't be home. Jenny helped set up three trays with silver, iced-tea glasses, and plates for some of Leona's leftover boysenberry pie. When the sun had dropped behind the trees and the terrace was reasonably cool, she carried them outside to a table beside the pool.

It was pleasant dining out of doors, a custom prohibited by the dust in Tokyo. Alan was very courteous to Mrs. Smith, remembering to pull out her chair and pass her the sugar first, and Jenny was proud of him. She felt relaxed and happy, and for the first time since she had left her parents she wasn't homesick at all.

Later, after her grandmother had returned to the coolness of the house to finish a book she was reading, Alan said to Jenny, "A cousin of mine is being married next Saturday. It's a four o'clock wedding, and I'd like you to go with me."

"But I haven't been invited. I don't know him," Jenny protested.

"It's a she—Lucille Dexter—and she told me I could bring a girl. I'm inviting you."

"Well—" Jenny hesitated. "I must speak to Grandmother."

"She knows the Dexters. She may even be going herself."

It turned out that this was the case, and Mrs. Smith was quite agreeable to Alan's proposal. "I think it will be interesting for Jenny to see an American wedding," she said, with a barely perceptible edge of bitterness to her voice.

Jenny was too excited to be aware of any brusqueness in her grandmother's manner. "What will I wear?" she asked Alan, when they were alone once more.

"I don't know. Ask Janet. What would you wear to a wedding in Tokyo?"

"Oh, at home for special occasions we wear a kimono," Jenny replied promptly.

Alan's eyes twinkled. "Have you got a kimono here?"

"Ye-es." Jenny sounded doubtful.

"There's your answer!" Alan cried. "You'll be a sensation. Promise me now!"

"I'm not sure—" Jenny paused, unwilling to confess that she was not sure her grandmother would like it. Yet every impulse inclined her to please Alan. How could any girl refuse the urgency in his voice? "Very well. I promise," she said very seriously.

Afterward she was sorry she had been so impulsive, because now it became doubly difficult to mention the matter to her grandmother. She was committed by her word to Alan. So what would she do if her grandmother disapproved?

Again Jenny acted in a typically Japanese fashion. Instead of meeting the problem head on, as Janet Carlisle would have done, she avoided the subject completely, and for a wonder her grandmother didn't inquire what she intended to wear. Instead, she asked, "Have you something suitable?" And Jenny murmured a meek, but quite positive, "Yes."

It was with a strange mixture of daring and guilt—for why was either emotion necessary?—that Jenny went up to her room to dress at three o'clock Saturday afternoon. Never before had she attempted to put on a kimono without her mother's help, and she was sure she would need at least half an hour to get into the outfit properly.

Midori, having been raised in pre-war Japan, could arrange the complicated costume without even looking in the mirror, even tying the *obi,* a stiff wraparound sash with a complicated bow in the back, by herself. But Jenny was of the post-war generation, who wore kimonos only for very special occasions, like a wedding or a special holiday, and she was far from expert. Luckily there was a long mirror on the bathroom door, because only with its aid could she be sure that she would be presentable.

Taking the kimono from its tissue-paper wrapping, Jenny found it impossible to feel anything but festive. The colors of the flowers strewn over the pale-blue silk were bright and cheerful—lavender wisteria, yellow chrysanthemums, pink bush clover, green pampas grass—all gloriously combined in harmonious Japanese style. Jenny laid it out on the bed while she slipped into white cotton socks called *tabi*, with a separation between the toes to accommodate the strap of the sandals she would wear. The platform soles of these *zori* made Jenny a full inch taller, so that her image in the mirror seemed different and interesting as she adjusted the long garment, fashioned just like the outer kimono, which served as underwear.

The kimono itself was very long. It trailed on the floor, so that until Jenny tucked it up around her waist, she looked like a little girl dressing up in her mother's clothes. Turning, she checked the length—just to her ankles—then made sure that each of the three strings with which she tied it—one around her hips, one around her waist, and one around her chest—were fastened so tightly they couldn't possibly slip.

No hooks or pins—and certainly no zipper!—were used with this traditional costume. Concealing the unflattering strings was the nine-inch-wide *obi*, of stiff, heavy brocade, woven with gilt thread. Usually Midori arranged Jenny's *obi*, winding it around her chest again and again and finally tying it so that it looked as though a butterfly had alighted on her back. Alone, however, Jenny could never have achieved the proper effect, so Midori had fashioned a special sash with a pre-tied bow.

An "instant *obi*" they had called it, as they worked on it together, cheating a little, because here they used hooks and eyes. "Like instant coffee and all the other instant things in the United States," Jenny had said in amusement. "I wonder what my American grandmother will think of this?"

She still wondered, as she slipped a silk-covered rectangle of cardboard, with a pocket for a handkerchief or fan, out of sight between the *obi* and the kimono. Then she turned back to the mirror, moving her arms experimentally, to get the full effect of the long sleeves waving gracefully around her knees. Although she had never felt more feminine, she also felt somewhat timid, and had a dawning awareness that it would take a certain amount of courage to appear among all these Americans in traditional Japanese dress.

Yet she had promised Alan, and she was glad that he would see her in the customary garment of her mother's ancestors. She wasn't ashamed that she was half Japanese; she was proud of it! And in a way the wearing of the kimono would be her statement of independence, an unspoken declaration to her American grandmother that she intended to remain Jenny Kimura—Jenny *Kimura* Smith!

Raising her hands and lifting her shining hair from her shoulders, Jenny let it fall behind her back in a straight black sweep. She was unaware that she thrust out her chin pugnaciously as she did so, in direct imitation of her father. When she lowered her arms again she looked every inch a pretty and defenseless girl.

There was a knock at the door. "Miss Jenny, your grandmother says you'd best hurry. It's gettin' mighty late and weddin's don't wait!"

"I'm coming, Leona." As Jenny walked out into the hall the maid fell back in astonishment. "My land!" she exclaimed. "My land, if you don't look gorgeous, like you was goin' to a fancy-dress ball!"

Jenny gulped. "Sh!" she warned. "I want to surprise Grandmother."

"You'll surprise her all right!" Leona said.

There was no misinterpreting her meaning, but Jenny could not turn back now. Mischievously, but without smiling, she winked. Then she went, with short, shuffling steps that accommodated the movement of her body to the long, tight robe, through the hall and down the carpeted stairs.

If she had planned a stage entrance she couldn't have succeeded more theatrically. But from her audience of two, the reaction was not a storm of applause. Alan, it was true, smiled his delighted approval and stepped forward to greet her, but Jenny's grandmother stifled a gasp and her eyes glazed with dismay. For a single horrified instant Jenny feared that she might burst into tears as she had that night at the airport. Instead, she glanced at her watch.

"No," she said, "there's no time to change."

"How marvelous!" Alan exclaimed simultaneously. "You look like Madame Butterfly!"

Mrs. Smith turned, her lips in a straight, rigid line.

"A decidedly inappropriate remark," she said with a lift of her eyebrows. "I'm sorry, Jennifer, that you didn't see fit to consult me, but if this is the way you want it, so be it. I just hope you won't be sorry. That is all I have to say."

Now I'm supposed to cringe like a whipped puppy, thought Jenny belligerently. Well, I won't do it. She can't intimidate me. Although it was breaking all rules of Japanese etiquette, she made no attempt to reply or to apologize, for what was there to apologize for?

The drive to the church was mercifully brief. Mrs. Smith pretended to concentrate on her driving, and Jenny sat miserably between her grandmother and Alan on the front seat. Her stomach, squeezed by the unaccustomed *obi*, developed a tendency to gurgle, and her mouth felt parched. Homesickness rose in her throat like an attack of nausea, and she couldn't even feel glad that Alan had been admiring. She wanted to die. If she had been a *samurai* warrior she would have fallen on her sword!

It was difficult to find a place to park, the street was so crowded with long, polished cars, but eventually they joined the latecomers hurrying toward the Gothic doorway that led into the Episcopal gloom of a crowded nave. Jenny was conscious of white peonies in two great vases flanking the altar, of an offered arm, and of her progress with the usher down an aisle between whispering voices.

"Who is she?"

"Charming!"

103

"My dear, Jennifer Smith's granddaughter! Good heavens, look at Jennifer's face!"

Eyes straight ahead, Jenny heard not a word. She was concentrating on keeping control of her stomach. Suppose it should gurgle, out loud, right here in church!

"Friends of the bride," her grandmother had said, and they were seated accordingly, Mrs. Smith entering the pew first, followed by Jenny, with Alan sitting on the aisle. Jenny was grateful to be partially concealed from the curious. She glanced at Alan to see how he was bearing up, and, with a sudden gesture of encouragement, the boy reached over and gave her hand a brief squeeze.

Turning to him, Jenny smiled wanly, then gave a quick look at her grandmother to make sure the gesture had gone unobserved. In a flash of total recall she could see herself again at the age of five, on the day of the Doll Festival, again dressed in a kimono. Her father had invited some American friends to the house for the celebration, and they had brought along a son about Jenny's age. Someone had suggested taking snapshots, and she had been required to hold hands with the strange child. She could see herself, standing before the niche called a *kakemono,* crimson with embarrassment, although he had been quite handsome. But not as handsome as Alan Carlisle.

The organist was playing a processional, and the bridesmaids were appearing, pacing jerkily, as though they were mechanically operated. Then came the maid of honor, a beautiful blonde, and finally the bride, with lowered eyes, secure on her father's arm. Jenny forgot her own misery as she gazed at the floating veil, the pure, sweet line of the wedding gown, and modesty of the girl's demeanor. This was something Midori should have seen! This she would have loved and understood.

The ceremony was high church, with the priest in black cassock and embroidered white linen. The words he spoke were strange to Jenny, but solemn and impressive. When the bride handed her bouquet to the maid of honor and her father stepped back to give place to the young groom she was touched and gladdened. A couple united, a home founded, the hope of children to come. . . .

The responses were not halting, but quiet and firm. The benediction was said, and suddenly the triumphant strains of the recessional awakened Jenny from her reverie. Like every girl who has ever attended a wedding, she had been envisioning her own.

The elapsed time, she realized, had calmed her. By the time she left the church, walking down the stone steps with Alan while her grandmother lingered, trapped by an ancient lady with a hearing aid, Jenny had recovered her surface composure. The curious eyes turned on her were more often than not accompanied by pleasant smiles. Naturally people were inquisitive, but they were also kind.

The reception was held at the country club on a huge terrace covered by a canvas marquee. Negro waiters were passing trays of champagne, and as Jenny waited with Alan to go through the receiving line she kept glancing at them, still as fascinated as she had been by the porters at the air terminal. "Aren't they handsome?" she whispered to Alan. "Such wonderful dark, shining skin!"

He laughed at her as though she were a precocious child, and presented her proudly to his relatives, who looked too preoccupied to be astonished. Then the groom said, "You make our wedding even more festive by your costume," and Jenny felt repaid for any embarrassment she might have caused her grandmother.

As a matter of fact, as Alan had promised, she created a mild sensation. Young people gathered round, anxious to be introduced, and stayed to admire Jenny's kimono and ask her questions about Japan, which obviously seemed very remote and romantic to most of them.

Mrs. Smith, quite naturally, was embraced by members of her own age group. While the young people gathered for refreshments on the terrace, their elders sought the comparative comfort of the air-conditioned reception rooms.

There was an orchestra for dancing, and a huge tiered wedding cake from which the bride cut the first slice while a candid-cameraman snapped pictures. There were ice cream, tea and coffee, finger sandwiches, and fancy cookies, and an informality and gaiety that Jenny found irresistible. In Japan the older people would have been more conspicuous; here the wedding reception seemed planned with the young in mind.

The roving photographer circled around Jenny and took snapshots from all angles, as though she interested him almost as much as the bride. Embarrassed, she tried to shrink into the background, but her kimono made this impossible. Janet Carlisle, in a white dress that contrasted delightfully with her suntan, came up and suggested a tennis game for Monday morning. John Sears, who had managed to get a haircut since the night of the cookout, appeared at Jenny's side and asked how she was getting on.

"Just fine," Jenny said, smiling to thank him for his interest.

"Well, it sure must be different."

"Oh, it is!" Jenny replied. "But I enjoy your funny customs! Like all the bridesmaids' dressing alike and the ushers' wearing gardenias and gloves. They make a wedding delightful. I'm having a lovely time."

It was true. As she became caught up in the kaleidoscopic festivities, Jenny all but forgot her grandmother's disapproval. This was something she wouldn't have missed for anything! When Alan led her over to meet his mother she was smiling happily, entertained by everything she saw and pleased to have been included in such a typically American celebration.

The introduction was simple. "Mother, this is Jenny Kimura Smith, the girl I've been telling you about."

"Oh yes!" Mrs. Carlisle, a slender, fashionably dressed woman, who looked far too young to have a son as old as Alan, smiled and shook hands. Then, because she was wearing a kimono and it seemed quite natural, Jenny bowed.

"I know your grandmother only slightly," said Mrs. Carlisle, "but I understand your visit has quite enhanced the summer for our young people. How nice to have you with us, my dear."

"Thank you. I like being here," Jenny said. "Everyone has been very kind." Then she added impulsively, "Especially Alan. He has taken me to so many interesting places in these last two weeks!"

Mrs. Carlisle's eyebrows lifted. "Aha!" she said, glancing at her son with amused accusal. "So that's why you're never home!" She turned back to Jenny. "You must get him to bring you to dinner some evening. Let me see. What about next Tuesday night?"

"I think that would be lovely," Jenny said, her eyes sparkling, "unless my grandmother has other plans."

"We'll expect you then," replied Mrs. Carlisle, still smiling. "Alan can stop by for you about six."

✿ EIGHT

Although she continued to enjoy herself at the wedding reception, Mrs. Carlisle's invitation to dinner was the climax of the afternoon for Jenny. She watched from the background as the bride tossed her bouquet to the girls gathered at the foot of the main staircase, and was glad when the prettiest of the bridesmaids caught it. She accepted a handful of rice and another of confetti when Alan pressed them upon her, but felt quite baffled. "What do I do with this?"

"You throw it at them."

"At the bride and groom?"

Alan nodded.

"Won't they mind?"

"They expect it," Janet Carlisle assured Jenny. "It's to wish them good luck."

A murmur swept the young people standing on the country-club steps. "Here they come!" The bride, in a beige traveling suit, burst out of the door to run across the terrace hand in hand with the groom, then slowed and half hid her face in her husband's shoulder as the guests began to pelt the newlyweds with confetti and rice. An instant later they were in a waiting car, leaning out of the window together and waving good-bye, while cameras and members of the wedding party called last-minute best wishes. Jenny watched quietly, smiling at the happy nonsense and trying to capture every detail so that she could tell Yukari.

"It is all so very gay!" she said to John Sears, whom she found at her elbow. "Such terrible extravagance, to throw away rice!"

John nodded, but looked as though he were lost for an answer, so Jenny went off in search of her grandmother, whom she felt she had neglected far too long. Besides, she must make sure that on Tuesday evening she'd be free to go to the Carlisles.

Mrs. Smith was on the lookout also. "Oh, there you are," she said, as Jenny broke away from the throng of tall American young people. "I think it's about time to go home."

Jenny acquiesced immediately, aware that her grandmother looked very weary. Lines radiated from the corners of her eyes and her usually firm mouth drooped. "I'll go tell Alan we're leaving," Jenny said.

"So early?" Alan asked, a trifle dismayed. He glanced toward the doorway where his aunt and uncle were bidding a few older guests good-bye. "Why don't you tell Mrs. Smith I'll bring you home? I really ought to hang around a while, being a relative and all."

Jenny hesitated, rather tempted, but remembered

her grandmother's worn face. "I think I'd better go on," she decided. "Grandmother seems tired. But you stay, please, Alan. Actually, I think it would be better if I went home with her alone."

The boy demurred, but finally let Jenny go, although he escorted the pair to Mrs. Smith's car and helped them in. "You're sure you don't mind?" he asked at the very last minute. "You're sure you don't want me to come along?"

"No indeed!" Jenny insisted, serene in the knowledge she would be seeing him soon again. "I think you really *should* stay, since it's a family affair."

Mrs. Smith made no comment, and Jenny thought that her good-bye was rather cold. They had no sooner turned out of the country-club drive than her grandmother commented, rather sharply, "When a boy invites you somewhere, Jennifer, he should also take you home. Alan was quite out of order in this instance, and you shouldn't have encouraged his bad manners."

Jenny's ebullience drained away like air from a leaky balloon. Quite deflated, she made herself very small and murmured, "I'm sorry, Grandmother. I didn't understand."

"There are a great many things you don't understand, my dear," said Mrs. Smith relentlessly. "That is quite obvious, or you never would have worn that costume to an afternoon wedding. You look as though you were dressed for a Halloween party. It was most inappropriate."

Tears started in Jenny's eyes. She felt crushed and deeply offended. Nobody she had talked to seemed to find her kimono inappropriate. They had been interested and, for the most part, openly admiring.

Gathering her courage, Jenny said, "At home wearing a kimono is a sign of respect. We dress up for weddings and big parties. Please excuse me if I was wrong."

The last sentence, spoken in a whisper, barely reached her grandmother's ears. Frowning at the road in concentration, Mrs. Smith picked up the last word and said, "Not wrong, exactly. Thoughtless. As though you have no idea of my position—of how critical people can be."

Jenny felt nonplussed. "You mean they criticize *you* because I wear a kimono?"

Mrs. Smith ran her tongue over her lips nervously. "Not everyone," she admitted. "But there are enough. This isn't New York or Boston. This is the Middle West."

Jenny sat without speaking, and after a few seconds her grandmother said, "Gordon should have told you there would be a certain amount of intolerance. He grew up here. He knows perfectly well what a storm he raised." Still Jenny waited, and her grandmother continued, "An interracial marriage is very unusual, Jenny, *very* unusual in Kansas City. In fact, unheard of among my friends. Our fathers and husbands worked hard to establish not only a business, but social position. It isn't easy to see the next generation tear it to shreds."

Jenny wished wildly that she could disappear into thin air. I thought she was getting used to me, but it's no better than it was in the beginning. She still can't accept the fact that I'm part Japanese!

"Why did you invite me here?" she asked, when she could trust herself to speak. "You waited sixteen years. Why now?"

Mrs. Smith seemed to shrink, to lose stature. Her shoulders slumped and her hands looked withered as they clutched the wheel. "Oh, Jenny, my dear," she cried, "it isn't your fault, any of it. Forgive me! I'm getting old—I miss Gordon more each year—I had to try!"

Compassion flooded Jenny, washing away some of the bitterness in her mouth. Little as she might understand her, this was a tragic woman, marble-hearted at one moment, abject the next. But how could she, Jenny, atone for a sin never committed? How could she hope to change an attitude developed during a lifetime?

She said, "Grandmother, I'm sorry to have disappointed you. If you want to send me home—" Jenny couldn't go on. Leave Alan? Leave this aging, lonely woman? Leave this big, fascinating country, still unexplored?

Her grandmother turned into the drive, pulled on the brake, and lurched to a stop. "Nonsense!" she said brusquely. "Let's forget the whole thing. We're both overtired and emotional. Go put on a bathing suit and we'll have a swim."

A swim—the panacea for every upset! If Jenny hadn't been so disturbed she would have recognized the humor of the suggestion. As it was, she was numb, desensitized. In Japan such a conversation would have been fatal to any further relationship. Even here it would leave a permanent scar.

Climbing the stairs slowly, Jenny went to her room and shut the door, leaning against it weakly. She was filled with an overwhelming desire to see her mother, to hear her speak some of her gentle words of Buddhist wisdom. All her life Jenny had been taught to act in moderation. "Never expose your deepest feelings," Midori had cautioned. "Never say things you may regret." And again, "To exist is to suffer." How true!

Jenny undressed, aware that it was a relief to be rid of the corseting *obi*, to kick off the thonged sandals, and to slip out of the hot cotton socks. Chilled by the sudden return to air-conditioning, she shivered, and fought a desire to ignore her grandmother's latest order. All she really wanted to do was to crawl into bed.

Still, a swim did clear the air to a certain extent. Now that Jenny could dive in from the deep end and negotiate the length of the pool, she had a sense of achievement that could not be denied. Her grand-mother, watching her, clapped her hands in approval and congratulated her on her newfound skill as though nothing had happened, and together they sat on the stone coping and let the last rays of the setting sun caress their shoulders and necks.

After a while Jenny ventured to say, "Mrs. Carlisle has invited me for dinner Tuesday evening. May I go?"

Her grandmother looked both surprised and pleased. "Of course!"

With a sigh of relief Jenny said, "Thank you," and her spirits began to lift. With Tuesday to look forward to, the future didn't seem quite so intolerable.

During the next three days Jenny did her best to be the obedient granddaughter, and Mrs. Smith attempted to be less critical and tense. She took her young guest shopping, buying her some Bermuda shorts and a bright cotton dress that Jenny considered "very American." Slowly the rift between the two began to heal.

Alan, meanwhile, continued his attentions, dropping by whenever possible. Leona spoiled him by baking large batches of his favorite butterscotch brownies, and Mrs. Smith seemed gratified that Jenny had found such an acceptable companion.

"Your boy friend," Leona called him, when Jenny and she were alone. "Didn't I tell you, right from the start, you were bound to make a hit?"

"Oh, Leona, stop teasing!" Jenny would complain, but actually she enjoyed the maid's good-humored banter. Since she could scarcely discuss Alan with Janet Carlisle, his own sister, Leona came to take the place of Yukari in Jenny's life. On Tuesday morning, consequently, she consulted Leona on what she should wear to dinner. "My new dress, do you think?"

"Your new dress is mighty pretty," Leona said. "Or I could press your white linen. That's right becoming, too, with your dark skin and hair."

This reference to her coloring decided Jenny against

115

the maid's suggestion. Tonight she wanted to look American, not Japanese. Besides, wearing something new always made her feel special, and she wanted the evening to be a thoroughgoing success.

Her grandmother seemed pleased by the choice. "You look very sweet," she said, when Jenny came downstairs just before six o'clock. Appearing from the kitchen, Leona stood in the hall drying her hands on a dish towel and adding the reinforcement of her approval. "Like a little lady! That's right."

Jenny thanked them gratefully. She needed their reassurance, because her heart was pumping wildly. It was so unutterably exciting to be invited to a boy's home! Why, in Tokyo such a thing would be tantamount to announcing an engagement, and surely here it could not be without importance. Otherwise, why would both her grandmother and Leona be so pleased?

Alan was slightly late. Waiting for him, Jenny prowled the downstairs rooms, inspecting herself critically in every mirror she passed. The deep-piled rugs, the colorful curtains and upholstery, the shining brasses on the antique chests, and the tinted walls were all familiar to her now, but they never failed to give her a feeling that she was walking through a dream, because they were all so very different from anything she had ever known. Would the Carlisles have a house like this? she wondered, for the first time curious about the place in which Alan lived.

As it turned out, the Carlisles lived in quite a different style from that of Jenny's grandmother. Their one-story house was contemporary in design, with sliding glass doors opening out from a combination living room and dining room to a grove of tall, spindly trees. Beyond was a glimpse of green grass, flanking a concrete-lined runnel, which was quite dry this evening but which, Alan assured her, became a fast-running brook after a heavy rain.

Both Mr. and Mrs. Carlisle, as well as Janet, seemed resigned to the ridiculous concrete facing that confined the brook. "There once was a politician named Pendergast," declaimed Alan's father, as though he were reading from a textbook, "who wished to build Kansas City in his own image. This is the result."

Because Mr. Carlisle was the one member of the family Jenny had not previously met, she went to special pains to make conversation with him, a stocky, square man wearing bifocals, through which he peered at her in solemn concentration.

"I understand you're called Jenny Kimura," he said almost at once. "What does Kimura mean in English?"

"It's just a family name, like Smith—or Carlisle."

"But doesn't it have some meaning?"

"Well, literally translated, it means 'tree village,'" Jenny said. "But it isn't a special sort of name like Kajuro, for instance, which means 'delightful things are doubled' in Japanese."

"How quaint!" exclaimed Mrs. Carlisle, who was going to and fro from the kitchen. "It must be fascinating to live in a world so different from ours."

"It's your world that seems different to me," admitted Jenny. She spread her arms. "The space, the freedom—it's wonderful!"

117

"Jenny's becoming so acclimated she'll never want to go home," suggested Janet teasingly.

"Oh, I'm not so sure about that," said Mr. Carlisle pleasantly. "Once a Japanese, always a Japanese, eh?"

"You forget, Pop," broke in Alan, "that Jenny's only *half* Japanese."

"Oh dear!" Mr. Carlisle thumped his head. "Somebody did tell me. Excuse me, child. It's just that you look so—so Oriental somehow. Not that it's a handicap, mind you. You're very pretty—you are indeed!"

Alan's mother, who was lighting candles on the dinner table, frowned and bit her lip, whether from concentration or annoyance Jenny couldn't tell. So she asked, "May I help you?" more to change the subject than from a feeling that she was needed. But her hostess shook her head. "Thanks, but Janet and I can manage quite nicely, my dear."

In spite of Jenny's desire to melt unobtrusively into the family surroundings, the dinner-table conversation remained concerned with Japan. Mr. Carlisle prodded Jenny for information concerning the postwar changes in the economy of the islands, questioned her concerning her father's business, and even touched on religion, saying, "I suppose you're a Buddhist or Shinto. Never could quite keep in mind the difference between the two."

Jenny Kimura couldn't help laughing, because the remark was so naïve. "My mother's family are Buddhists," she said. "Shinto isn't quite a religion, you see, although there are shrines everywhere. People often stop to say a prayer or make a wish." She smiled at

118

Alan. "In much the same way you wish on a hay wagon or on a star."

Intercepting the look between Jenny and her son, Mrs. Carlisle's eyes widened. "How nice that our children have had a chance to know you," she said brightly. "It's so good for them to have these contacts, isn't it, Harold? No matter how remote."

Startled, Jenny sat a little straighter. She hadn't felt remote, until this minute. She'd felt welcomed, even embraced, by Alan's family. Now, abruptly, she was an outsider again.

"Good grief, Mother, what do you mean remote? No part of the world's remote anymore, not even Patagonia!" Janet, sounding embarrassed, glanced at her brother, who was frowning in apparent concentration at some peas that kept slipping off his fork. Then she caught Jenny's eye and smiled comfortingly. "Mummy's kind of old-fashioned in some ways."

Mrs. Carlisle didn't look old-fashioned, however. Her hairdo and her clothes seemed to Jenny, now as at the wedding, in the height of style. Her figure was trim, almost girlish, and her poise was unshakable. "I'm discussing the two cultures, darling," she retorted lightly. "You must admit they are poles apart." Suddenly she leaned forward, resting her elbows on the table, and said, "Tell me, Jenny, is your father really resigned to living over there?"

The question was so unexpected that Jenny answered it quite spontaneously. "Resigned? I don't know what you mean. He's happy in Tokyo. It's his home."

Mrs. Carlisle shook her head. "It's beyond me. I'll

admit it's beyond me. But then *we* all probably seem odd to you."

Sometimes you do, Jenny wanted to say, sensing she was being baited, but conventional politeness stood in the way. "No, you seem quite normal," she replied with a smile. "After all, Daddy isn't *that* different. He's still American."

The doorbell rang, and Janet pushed back her chair and went to answer it, murmuring, "That's Nick Abell. He's taking me to a hootenanny. I've got to run." She said hurried good-byes, calling back over her shoulder, "Leave the dishes, Mother. I'll do them when I come back."

But when Janet had gone and Alan had vanished into the yard with his father, who needed his help in repairing a leaky outside faucet, Jenny Kimura begged, "May I take Janet's place? I'm getting quite handy around Grandmother's kitchen. You'd be surprised."

Mrs. Carlisle accepted the offer without hesitation. Indeed, she seemed pleased at the opportunity to chat with Jenny alone and, instead of continuing the discussion of Japan, began to talk about her own children.

"Janet's wonderful with youngsters," she told Jenny. "I think she'd make a splendid nursery-school teacher, if only she doesn't get married as soon as she leaves school."

"Will she go on to college?" Jenny Kimura asked. It was a question she was asking herself also these days, because the thought of returning to the States when high school was over presented itself as an exciting possibility.

Mrs. Carlisle shrugged. "Junior college, maybe. Education isn't so important, is it, for a pretty girl?" She didn't seem to expect an answer, but hurried on. "For a boy, though, it's paramount, and we're so happy about Williams for Alan. New England will be a pleasant change, and of course Williamstown is handy to Smith and Bennington and any number of girls' schools. He should have a wonderful time!"

"I'm sure he will," murmured Jenny, but she felt uneasy. "Alan seems very bright."

"Oh, he is," agreed his mother confidently. "I have such high hopes for him!" She turned off the faucet under which she had been rinsing dinner plates, and said confidentially, "I just hope he makes a good marriage—a really *good* marriage—to a girl of his own background and his own class." Then she twisted the handle of the faucet so that water gushed out once more. "That's always wisest, don't you think?"

This time an answer was expected, but Jenny felt at a loss. "I think he should do what will make him happiest," she said finally, aware of the tension increasing between her and her hostess, who seemed determined to engage her in a kind of double talk.

This response made Mrs. Carlisle laugh gaily. "You sound so young," she chided. "So very young and romantic and full of illusions, just like Alan. Each new girl he discovers is always the greatest, but of course it will be years before he can possibly take one of them seriously."

121

Now there was no mistaking Mrs. Carlisle's intent. Jenny's eyes darkened with anguish, but she was facing an adversary at whom she could not strike back. Instead she addressed her attention to the glasses she was arranging in the dishwasher, while she fought to retain her self-control.

Later, driving her home, Alan challenged Jenny's morose silence. "What's the matter?" he asked. Then he suggested shrewdly, "Mother give you a hard time?"

"She doesn't like me," Jenny replied flatly.

"Oh, pay no attention," Alan advised airily. "She has a thing about her only son. Plans to marry me off to a gilt-edged debutante, or else."

Jenny shook her head. "You can't treat it that lightly."

"Maybe you can't, but I can!" retorted Alan with a show of belligerence. "Come on, Jenny," he wheedled. "Forget it. Be yourself!"

Be yourself. It was a phrase her mother had often used in giving Jenny advice, but now on Alan's lips it sounded superficial and wrong. Suddenly all of Jenny's pent-up emotion came to a boiling point. She couldn't talk back to her grandmother, she couldn't fight Mrs. Carlisle, but she didn't have to take a scolding from Alan. He wasn't a grown-up!

"Be yourself!" Jenny scoffed, pounding her knees with clenched hands. "That's not what you mean, any of you. What you're trying to say is, 'Be more like us. Be American, and then maybe we'll let you play!' "

"Jenny!" Instead of being sympathetic, Alan sounded aggrieved.

122

"I don't care! I'm tired of being treated like a curiosity," Jenny cried bitterly. "At home my Japanese grandparents despise my father, because he's Caucasian. Over here people are shocked because my mother's Japanese. Where does that leave *me?*"

Appalled by this uncharacteristic outburst and unable to give a comforting answer, Alan could only retaliate in kind. "Oh, quit having a temper tantrum," he muttered irritably, as he turned into the Smith driveway. "I can't stand girls who make scenes!"

✿ NINE

It was a quarrel—a real quarrel! Jenny cried herself to sleep in a torment of self-castigation. Never before in her whole life had she spoken out so angrily. And to have made Alan the scapegoat of her indignation—Alan whom she adored! It was inexcusable.

When she awakened in the morning Jenny felt as though she had been whipped. Her eyes were half closed, the lids were swollen, and each breath was tremulous. How could she face her grandmother? How could she face Leona? How could she face anybody ever again?

It was possible to dawdle around her room until midmorning, because there was no regular breakfast schedule in the Smith house. But eventually Jenny had to creep downstairs and brave the inevitable questions about her evening at the Carlisles'. She had to pretend—what could she pretend?—that she had acquired a sudden eye infection? In that case, her grandmother would immediately call a doctor, and that would never do!

Then Jenny remembered with relief that Wednesday was her grandmother's Gray Lady day at the hospital. She'd have six hours of respite before the inquisition, and during this time she might manage to pull herself together and put up a decent front. Leona she could face; Leona was simple and understanding. If Leona realized that Jenny had been crying she wouldn't pry.

Sitting in the sunny kitchen with her face in the shadow, Jenny choked down the food the maid put before her and felt slightly better, but on the spur of the moment she pretended to feel ill. "I think I'll go back and lie down," she apologized.

Leona immediately approved. "You do that, honey. You look real peaked. Why don't you just get undressed and go back to bed. I'll bring up your meals on a tray."

The ruse was successful. Mrs. Smith accepted her granddaughter's indisposition as perfectly normal, and about four o'clock tiptoed in to ask if there was anything Jenny needed and tiptoed out again without even bringing up the subject of the previous evening. Luckily everybody in Kansas City goes out so much that one engagement more or less seems unimportant, Jenny thought.

To everyone but me!

How could she make amends? she wondered, as she regained a little perspective. Call Alan up? No, that would be too public and even perhaps improper. Write him a note? That seemed more plausible, but words of apology would be hard to find. Then a wonderful idea occurred to her. Suppose Alan were sorry, too. He might, conceivably, make the first move.

At this possibility Jenny brightened. She went into the bathroom, washed her face, brushed her hair, and put on lipstick, even though she didn't intend to see Alan if he dropped by. She would hide behind the screen of her indisposition and put him off until tomorrow, when she would look presentable once more.

Lying propped on pillows, Jenny turned the pages of a magazine and listened for the familiar sound of a rackety engine, but the clock hands crawled to five o'clock, then to six. Still, he might telephone, and this thought renewed her hope. If all else failed, she could still write the note.

Leona came in with an omelet, a green salad, and a cup custard about six-thirty. "You'd best not have anything heavy," was her opinion. "Tomorrow you'll feel better if you eat light tonight." Then she took an envelope from her pocket. For a moment Jenny's heart leaped, but the maid said, "This came for you in the afternoon mail. If you don't want the stamps I have a nephew who saves them, hear?"

Jenny tore them off the envelope at once, but not before she recognized Yukari's writing, the precise English-class penmanship, so familiar that it raised a lump in her throat. To her surprise, Yukari had written a whole letter in English rather than in the usual Japanese characters. Probably, Jenny suspected,

126

this was at the insistence of the teacher, who urged her students to practice at every opportunity.

Jenny propped the flimsy paper against the tray's edge and read as she ate:

Dear Jenny Kimura,

I was looking at map and suddenly got surprised to realize you in the other hemisphere. I still feel as if you would call me up at any moment and say, "Come to my house, Yukari. Daddy has bought me a new record again."

Jenny's eyes smarted with fresh tears, but she blinked them back, ashamed of her weakness. Yukari seemed so very dear.

I found at the airport you have a bold heart. (A bold heart? Ha! thought Jenny.) You looked as grand as a triumphant general when you walked up the stairs to the plane. I bet you can sleep very well snoring comfortably and eat quite a lot.

Well, how do you like the land of kettle and cowboys? Do you eat humburgers, hot dogs, and popcorns all the time? I heard that Americans eat too much steak and ice cream so they suddenly get fat. You had better be careful, if this is true.

Jenny thought, She's right. I've gained five pounds already, and my skirts feel tight around the waist. She put down her fork and pushed away the unfinished omelet. No time like the present to use self-control. Then she picked up the letter and read on:

What do you think of boys? Are they as handsome as Ricky Nelson? Have you talked to any yet?

Oh, if you only knew, thought Jenny. If you only knew! What she wouldn't give to have Yukari with her, right this minute, here in this room, a confidante she could trust. Her eyes blurred again in self-pity, so she picked at her salad for a few minutes until she could see to read the end:

It's raining almost every day in Tokyo. I can hardly wait for the sunny summer days. You don't have to worry about missing classes, I am taking all the notes for you.
Love,
Yukari

"Love, Yukari," Jenny murmured aloud. It all seemed so very long ago and far away—school, home, the girls with whom she had grown up. Then it occurred to her, in an instant of self-revelation, that she wouldn't trade places, even with her best friend. In spite of her misery, in spite of the feeling that this whole alien world was against her, Jenny Kimura was glad that she was not standing in Yukari's shoes, but in her own.

From that moment on, as though she had lived through the crisis of a severe illness, Jenny was aware

128

of a gradual improvement in her spirits. She slept fairly well, arose early the next morning, and went downstairs to find her grandmother lingering over a second cup of coffee, with a newspaper propped against the sugar bowl.

"Feeling better, dear?"

"Much better, thank you," Jenny replied with a show of confidence.

"Good, I've got a golf match at nine-thirty. Would you like to walk around with us?"

"I'd rather not this morning," Jenny demurred. "I really should write some letters, and—"

As she hesitated, her grandmother dismissed the subject with a wave of her hand. "I forgot to ask you, did you have a pleasant evening with the Carlisles?"

Jenny nodded. "It was very interesting," she said, avoiding the telling of the outright fib.

"You were home quite early. I had just turned out my light when you came in." Jenny nodded again, and addressed herself to her breakfast while Mrs. Smith glanced at her watch, then pushed back her chair in haste. "Are you playing tennis or anything, Jenny? In other words, will you be all right?"

"Quite all right." Jenny was relieved that the conversation was closed. Yet, when she was left alone, Leona having gone off for her "Thursday" right after breakfast, Jenny wandered through the house like a lost soul. What was Alan doing now, right this minute? Changing a tire? Operating the gas pump? Checking a car for oil? If only he'd phone! But during the working day he was completely occupied. There remained the hope that he'd drop by late this afternoon.

The hours dragged, and Jenny accomplished nothing. It was impossible to settle down to the routine of letter writing when life had come to a standstill and every minute seemed to tick by with maddening slowness. By four o'clock Jenny was wringing her hands. It took a real effort of will to get into a bathing suit and arrange herself beside the pool as though nothing in the world were the matter.

Still Alan neither appeared nor telephoned. Suppertime came and went, the evening hours progressed inexorably toward bedtime, and Jenny found it increasingly difficult to dissemble. She was filled with chagrin, which was replaced eventually by a heartsick emptiness.

"Where's your young man?" Leona inquired, when Alan still did not appear after work on Friday. "You-all got to scrappin'? Shame on you!"

Jenny couldn't reply. She shook her head and hurried out of the room, unable to make any answer at all.

Mrs. Smith was more tactful. She didn't press Jenny for an explanation until Saturday afternoon, when she came hurrying home from another golf match. "Jenny!" she called. "Jenny, come here! I want to talk to you."

She sounded so emphatic that Jenny quailed. With drooping shoulders, but with eyes that told nothing, she entered the study. "What is it, Grandmother?"

"Sit down," Mrs. Smith suggested, not unkindly. "I want you to tell me exactly what happened at the Carlisles' on Tuesday night."

130

The question was as unexpected as a pistol shot. "Why—why, nothing," Jenny murmured evasively. "I don't know what you mean."

"I think you do," said Mrs. Smith with her usual directness. "Alan hasn't showed up all week. Did you have a fight?"

"Sort of," Jenny admitted, her eyes downcast.

"What about?"

"It's too involved to explain."

"I'd like you to try."

Jenny shook her head, her throat constricted. There was nothing she could say.

"Please, honey!" Mrs. Smith seemed to sympathize with Jenny's embarrassment, but she persisted. "What did Mrs. Carlisle do to you? What did she say?"

Jenny was aghast. "How did you know?"

Her grandmother chuckled bitterly. "I wasn't born yesterday, my dear child."

Sinking down on the sofa, her hands clasped tightly in her lap, Jenny fell mute again. She and her grandmother were virtually strangers. How could she talk about such matters to her? How could she expose her heart?

"I think I can guess," Mrs. Smith said after a moment. "She warned you off, didn't she? She made it plain that you were an outsider, that she had other plans for Alan. Was that it?"

"It wasn't anything she *said* actually. It was the way she said it," Jenny murmured wretchedly.

"What about Alan? How did he react?"

"He wasn't there. He was in the yard with his father," Jenny replied.

"Oh, I see!"

Mrs. Smith got up from her desk chair to pace up and down the room. Her mouth was thin and tight and her eyes were smoky with rage. "It's not your fault, Grandmother," Jenny cried anxiously. "It's not your fault she doesn't like me."

"This is beyond endurance!" said Mrs. Smith furiously. "I must have lost my wits!" Suddenly, in unprecedented passion, she clenched her fist and pounded on the desk. "The snake!" she muttered, to Jenny's shocked astonishment. "The spiteful snake!"

✿ TEN

I've got to talk to Alan, thought Jenny frantically, I've got to find out what's so terribly wrong. Mystified by her grandmother's violence, she wanted to flee, but sat rooted to the edge of the sofa.

Mrs. Smith started pacing again. "I just heard about it by chance," she said, as though Jenny had asked her a question. "In the locker room at the club someone mentioned that Beth Carlisle had canceled a luncheon date. Then a mutual friend said, 'Oh, yes, didn't you know? She suddenly decided to close the house and take the children east.'"

Jenny shook her head in disbelief. "Alan wouldn't leave his gas-station job. He's got it all figured out how much money he'll earn by September first." Then she grabbed at another straw. "Besides, what would Mr. Carlisle do?"

"He's living in town at his club," replied Mrs. Smith with a shrug.

This had a ring of veracity, even to Jenny's ears. "But it's so sudden," she murmured. "There was no mention of any trip Tuesday night. Why—"

"Mrs. Carlisle finds the Kansas City heat unendurable." Mrs. Smith lingered over the last word and repeated it. "Unendurable." She turned and went back to her desk, then sat down and faced Jenny. "I did think Alan had more spunk," she said. "He might at least have phoned."

Jenny, from the depths of despair, was thinking the same thing, but she couldn't admit it. It was an unwritten rule that a girl must never acknowledge to an adult the depth of her feeling for a boy. "Alan and I had a disagreement, remember? Perhaps he thought I should have phoned him."

It was a lame excuse, and one that Mrs. Smith wouldn't accept for an instant. "Rubbish!" she said. "We may as well face facts, Jenny. Alan was whisked out of town for just one excellent reason. He was getting too interested in you."

The statement was so brutally honest that Jenny was forced to believe it. "I'm sorry, Grandmother," she said quaveringly. "I seem to be nothing but an embarrassment to you."

"Nonsense!" said Mrs. Smith in the same crisp manner in which she had just said "Rubbish!" She sat up straight and thrust her chin forward in a manner Jenny now recognized as a family characteristic. "Stop apologizing. Where's your pride?"

She's not talking to me; she's talking to herself, Jenny realized with a start. And in that moment her

134

grandmother seemed transformed. She was no longer a family figurehead; she was a person, a woman who was really just a grown-up girl, as emotionally involved in this predicament as was Jenny herself. Though in a different way, of course. Jenny felt torn apart, as she kept remembering Alan's warm smile and eager, glowing eyes. Her grandmother, on the other hand, was positively militant in her anger. For the first time Jenny realized that here was a woman, who, if driven to it, would leap to her defense.

I belong to her, Jenny thought. In spite of—or perhaps *because* of—everything, I belong to her! Suddenly, on an impulse that conquered her timidity, she jumped to her feet and went over to bury her head on her grandmother's shoulder. "I think you are a very wonderful person," she whispered from the bottom of her heart.

It was the beginning of a new affinity between the two, a sort of secret alliance, which they didn't discuss, even with one another. Mrs. Smith didn't again mention Alan Carlisle's name, and she hushed Leona the next time she started to tease Jenny about his absence. But when a special-delivery letter postmarked Chicago arrived on Sunday morning, she hurried to find Jenny. It was obvious she was relieved, even though she grumbled, "Well, it's about time."

Jenny carried the rather grubby envelope to her room so that she could open it in private. The message was short, scrawled in pencil on hotel stationery.

"Jenny dear," Alan had written. "Forgive me for

not calling you, but things suddenly got very tense at our house, with Mother threatening a nervous breakdown or something. The upshot of it is that we're heading east to visit my aunt and uncle on Bass River. For a month, maybe. But I'll see you when I get back. I promise. And, meanwhile, I'll keep in touch."

It wasn't much, but it was enough. It was evidence of good faith. And the "Jenny dear" was delightfully intimate, so much cozier than "Dear Jenny" would have been.

Holding the letter in trembling hands, Jenny read it again and again. "I'll see you. . . . I promise!" All was not lost, after all.

But the ensuing days were very lonely. Without Janet as a tennis partner, and without Alan's companionship in the long evenings, Jenny Kimura faded like a field flower plucked and abandoned by some thoughtless wayfarer. She caught up with her correspondence, wrote regularly in Yukari's gift diary, helped arrange flowers and do marketing, but she felt dull and bored. Retreating from the possibility of finding other friends, she slept more than usual, restlessly refused to settle down to any serious reading, and began to eat compulsively between meals, just for something to do.

Abruptly one morning Mrs. Smith came to a decision. "I think we'll leave for the Cape next week instead of waiting until the first of August," she said. "I'll phone Boston tonight and talk to my daughter-in-law. If young Richard can come along to the Cape with us a little earlier than we'd planned, there's no reason to rust away here. We can leave the first of next week."

Young Richard, as Jenny had been apprised, was her first cousin, the son of her father's dead brother. His widow, after an interval of several years, had remarried, and was now the wife of a Harvard professor named Russell Harrington.

"You'll like Virginia," Mrs. Smith promised her granddaughter. "She's very sensible and sympathetic." Then she grinned and added, "Not at all like me."

Jenny knew that this called for a smile, not a denial. "I'm anxious to meet my cousin, too. Richard." She tried out the name on her tongue.

"We usually call him Dick," said her grandmother absently. She was thinking of all the things that must be done before she could get off. "Mothballs," she said aloud. "Or whatever you call them. Kennel reservation for Freddy. Jenny, I think you'd better start making a list."

The activity was heartening, and for the next few days Jenny was so busy she didn't have time to mope. A postcard came from Alan, this time from Buffalo, New York, warning Jenny that he intended to "go over Niagara Falls in a barrell, just like some guy did a long time ago."

Jenny consulted her grandmother. "He's teasing?" she asked.

"Yes, he's teasing," Mrs. Smith replied. "Good heavens, child, look at the way he's spelled barrel. With two *l*'s. Truly, the schooling young people get today!"

It was only at times like this that Jenny felt her

137

grandmother seemed old—old and conventional to a degree that made her impatient. What difference did it make how Alan spelled a common English word, if he had an interesting personality? She couldn't understand why elderly people became so obsessed with details.

A few minutes later, however, realizing that Alan had given her no address to which she might write, Jenny became more critical. This was one detail she would have found convenient. As it stood, she had no way of getting in touch with Alan until some subsequent letter was forwarded from Kansas City to Cambridge, Massachusetts, where the Harringtons lived, or to Cape Cod. This, as she well knew, might take something more than a week.

Nevertheless, Jenny packed for the trip with a growing sense of adventure. It would be interesting to see something of New England, which sounded very different from Kansas, stern and rockbound and foggy in contrast to this omnipresent heat. It would be fun to meet an unknown cousin, especially a boy, and it would be novel to stay at an American inn beside the sea.

Jenny had never spent a vacation at a shore resort. Her family always went to the mountains, taking a summer house in Gotemba, on the skirts of Mount Fuji. Here, in a typical Japanese house with a rambling garden, Jenny had learned the pleasures of the country. She had been allowed to wander through the tea fields, to walk through the woods, where mushrooms and ferns abounded, and to go out in a rowboat with her father, although she couldn't swim.

Even now she could remember the joys of those childhood summers, when she had spent long, happy hours catching dragonflies and grasshoppers, making houses for them from discarded boxes, and keeping them for a few days as her pets. She could also, very dimly, remember the sound of guns being fired at a military base in the distance, and the scars of the war still visible in some of the nearby towns.

From now on Jenny would have another summer to remember, not quite so idyllic, but nevertheless interlaced with excitement. She might not be especially happy, but at least she was living! She wasn't sitting home like Yukari, marking time.

On the morning Jenny and her grandmother left for Boston the airport presented quite a different picture than it had on that memorable evening little more than a month ago. The red tiled floor, the aluminum telephone booths, and the great clumps of contemporary lighting fixtures no longer seemed so odd, and the lofty ceiling was less forbidding now that the place was buzzing with life. Businessmen hurried to and fro with briefcases; vacationists, weighed down with golf clubs and tennis rackets, crowded around the ticket desks; and a voice, carried to the farthest reaches of the airport by loudspeakers, announced the constant arrival or departure of planes.

It happened to be a flawlessly clear day, and Jenny, from a window seat, could look down on the United

139

States spread out like a relief map below. The route was interesting, allowing glimpses of two of the Great Lakes and thousands of acres of farmland, neatly divided into rectangles and squares. But it was Niagara Falls, an innocent-looking froth of white water miles below, that especially captured Jenny's attention. Here Alan had been, and from the nearby city of Buffalo, with its clutter of buildings that looked like mere toys from this distance, he had sent the postcard that was now riding in Jenny's purse.

A little later, as the great plane descended toward the Boston airport, Mrs. Smith pointed out the long neck of land that led down the south shore of Massachusetts toward Cape Cod. "Then we must be flying over the Atlantic Ocean," Jenny said with a start. A whole continent away from the Pacific! How very far from Tokyo she felt now!

Coming in, the jet skimmed so close to the water that Jenny gasped. Then, a second later, there was a reassuring jolt, the roar of the braking engines, and once more she was gathering up her belongings, preparing to disembark.

Nobody appeared at the Boston airport to meet them, nor did Mrs. Smith seem to expect anyone. "We'll take a taxi to Cambridge," she said.

In a yellow cab they were whirled through a long tunnel with walls that reminded Jenny of a tiled bathroom, then over a maze of elevated highways to Storrow Drive. Now the taxi sped along a macadam strip beside the Charles River, and Mrs. Smith pointed out the part of the city called the Back Bay, the tall

140

buildings clustered around the famed dome of the Massachusetts Institute of Technology, and finally the old red-brick buildings of Harvard University, serene and beautiful amid a rash of contemporary architecture.

The Harringtons lived in a square white house on a hill called Coolidge. It was surrounded by a clapboard fence. To Jenny's eyes, it looked nondescript from the outside, and from the inside too, except for the books. There were books everywhere, on the tables, on the walls, on the sofa, even on the radiators. It was as though the house were built around books, and for the first few minutes Jenny found it impossible to focus on the people who moved among them.

Then she really began to *see* her aunt, a stocky woman with short, tousled brown hair and a voice almost as deep as a man's. Jenny need not have worried about being welcome. Mrs. Harrington greeted her warmly, but her good humor was as offhand as though her niece had run in from across the street, not as though she had come halfway around the world. Professor Harrington was not home—"He's in Paris this week," his wife mentioned casually—but Dick came pounding down the uncarpeted stairs to greet his grandmother and his cousin from Tokyo. He pulled up short, like a Newfoundland puppy suddenly reaching a fence, and Jenny gathered a general impression of untidiness—shaggy brown hair, torn blue jeans, ragged sneakers, a T-shirt far from immaculate —but the hand that Dick held out was firm and hard, his voice was as deep as his mother's, and his eyes were dark and sparkling.

It was the eyes, always the eyes, that Jenny would remember forever about Dick Harrington. They're like Daddy's, Jenny thought, but more alive, more questioning. While her father's expression was genial, Dick's was curious. Jenny's heart leaped with excitement. What fun to have such a close relative who was also a boy she wanted to know!

There was one more member of the household, a twelve-year-old child named Laurie who was Dick's half sister. She was a sprite of a girl, dancing with eagerness, her long fair hair caught back in Alice-in-Wonderland fashion. She came in from the backyard with a cocker-spaniel puppy in her arms, and Jenny couldn't decide which of the two was more appealing. One thing was sure, however, their blond beauty exactly matched.

Dick carried the bags upstairs to the guest bedroom, which Jenny and her grandmother would share. It had none of the pristine perfection of Mrs. Smith's guest room in Kansas City. In fact, it was downright disorderly, and Dick had to remove several stacks of books from the window seat in order to find a place where the suitcases could be put down.

"Mom meant to get to this room, but she's up against a deadline," Dick explained. Hoisting a teetering pile of books into his arms and anchoring it with his chin, he started to back out of the room, then stopped to say, "She does reviews, you know."

Jenny had not known, but now her grandmother told

her that Virginia Harrington had once been an editor for a Boston publishing firm, but after Laurie's birth she had given up her job and turned to book reviewing, with such success that she was in demand by New York as well as Boston newspapers and magazines. "She's made quite a thing of it," Mrs. Smith said, as she pushed aside a row of wire hangers in the single closet. "Though I must say," she added with a whisper, "she's not much of a housekeeper. They do live in the most Bohemian style."

It was different certainly, but Jenny found the tumbled rooms inviting, because of the books. They were on an enormous variety of subjects, travel, history, art, cooking, science. "Choose as many as you want," Mrs. Harrington invited, "and take them along to the Cape. What are your interests, Jenny? Have you made up your mind yet what you want to do?"

Jenny fumbled for an answer, but ended by shaking her head. This was the sort of question that confused her, because she felt it should have been asked of a boy, not a girl.

"Well, you have a little time," her aunt said comfortingly. "Are you coming back to the States to college, or are you going to the university in Tokyo?"

"Tokyo University? I don't think I could get in." Jenny laughed. "It's awfully hard, you know, even for boys."

Mrs. Harrington grinned, running her hands through her hair and wrinkling her nose. "I have a strong feeling," she said in her pleasant growl, "that boys and girls aren't so different in potential when it comes to brains."

It was a novel idea to Jenny, as were many of her aunt's convictions. She felt that in Cambridge she had been dropped into a new intellectual climate, one that she found quite captivating, but in which she felt out of her depth.

Dick and his mother argued about anything and everything, from whether the lawn needed mowing to whether or not it was important for American astronauts to beat the Russians to the moon. At the dinner table they discussed the relative merits of Giotto's doors on the campanile in Florence and Rodin's controversial *Gates of Hell*. To Jenny's surprise, Laurie entered into many of these conversations, asking questions, offering opinions, and becoming thoroughly involved. Jenny felt ill-informed beside this child who was four years her junior. When Mrs. Harrington repeated her invitation to select some reading matter for the Cape, Jenny made sure to choose one book on science and another on art.

It was arranged that Mrs. Smith and her two grandchildren would borrow the smaller of the Harringtons' cars for the month they planned to spend in New England, so the next morning Dick loaded the little Hillman convertible with luggage, water skis, tennis rackets, and various packages of books, many of them French paperbacks. Like his mother, he seemed to have a catholic taste.

Jenny said good-bye to her Aunt Virginia regretfully, because she felt they were just getting acquainted, and she would have liked to bask longer in the atmosphere of the Coolidge Hill house. But Mrs. Smith was impatient to be off. She found her daughter-in-law's hit-and-miss housekeeping upsetting, and couldn't settle down in such a clutter. "I'm particular," she confessed to Jenny privately. "And particular people never make good visitors."

En route to Cape Cod, Dick suddenly decided that it was important for Jenny to see Plymouth and get a glimpse of the historic rock, because of its Pilgrim history. Mrs. Smith didn't demur, so Dick turned off the express highway and joined the heavy traffic crowding the main street of a New England town built beside a curving bay.

In time they came to a monument and a stone canopy supported by Doric columns, in the center of which was a large granite boulder enclosed by an iron fence. Dick parked the car and insisted that Jenny walk over to get a closer look, pointing out the engraving—1620—on the rock's face. "That's the year the *Mayflower* pulled in here," he told her. "Of course they can't be sure the Pilgrims first set foot on *this* rock, but it's a good memorial to the landing, nevertheless."

Jenny was more amused than impressed. She thought it was funny to see a gray rock kept in a cage, as though it were an animal, and was surprised that Dick seemed to take American history so seriously. Looking at the faces of the camera-hung tourists who were visiting the spot, Jenny could see that they were quite solemn. "Perhaps because your history is so very short, people tend to make much of it," she suggested, her eyes twinkling.

Dick frowned. "I don't know why you think it's so hysterical, people coming to look at a rock. After all, in Japan they have rock gardens, don't they? *Just* rocks, I mean. Isn't there a temple called Ryoanji, with a garden made of rocks and raked sand?"

Jenny nodded. "In Kyoto. But that is supposed to be very artistic. It is different, I think."

Dick refused to be mollified. He was offended that his young cousin wouldn't take American history seriously, and sulked until they got back to the super-highway again.

Still Jenny felt that she had made her point, and in a subtle manner the incident cemented her relationship with her cousin. It was the first time in her life Jenny had dared argue with a boy, but she felt sure that it was her prerogative, as a relative, to treat Dick with the same freedom his mother displayed. In return, Dick no longer tried to impress Jenny with his superiority.

As they neared the Sagamore Bridge and crossed over the Cape Cod Canal from the mainland to the eighty-mile-long finger of land stretching out to Provincetown, Mrs. Smith sat back and relaxed with a sigh of contentment. "I've been coming here for fifteen years," she told Jenny. "By now it seems like my second home."

With the car racing along a highway built down the center of the peninsula, Jenny kept wondering what could be attractive about mile after mile of scrub pine and sandy hills. Eventually, however, Dick turned off toward the south shore, and the landscape changed abruptly. Weathered shingle or white clapboard houses appeared beside the road. Rambler roses trailed over fences, ponds nestled in strips of woodland, and village churches of elegant simplicity raised their spires to the blue sky.

"This part of the Cape never changes," murmured Mrs. Smith. "Around Hyannis it's all built up and horrid, but here it's just the same."

The sky seemed to broaden ahead of the car, and suddenly Jenny saw the sea, the limitless Atlantic, stretching all the way to a horizon beyond which was Europe. "Oh, I'm going to like this!" she cried, craning her neck and clapping her hands like a child. "Oh, Grandmother, I'm going to love it!"

For a moment she forgot how much more wonderful it would have been if Alan rather than Dick had been at her side.

✿ ELEVEN

The rambling inn was set on a bluff at the end of a clipped green lawn, and surrounded by a cluster of cottages, sleeping quarters for the guests, each of which commanded a sweeping view of a pleasant bay, a fingerlike sandbar, and the ocean beyond. Like chickens around a mother hen, the cottages nestled close to the main building, which contained dining rooms and a comfortable, chintz-draped lounge.

Jenny, her grandmother, and Dick each had a small bedroom, and shared a bath and a living room with a wood-burning fireplace. "Do you know," Jenny exclaimed, "that before I came to Kansas City I'd only seen fireplaces in the movies? Japanese houses don't have them." She smiled teasingly at Dick. "But we have something you've never seen!"

"What's that?" Always eager for information, her cousin spoke quickly, but Jenny was slow in replying, because she was swept with nostalgia. "When I was a little girl we had a pit under our dining-room table where we used to burn charcoal. In the winter my mother covered the table with a heavy cloth, and when we sat eating dinner the warm coals would keep our feet comfortable. I remember one snowy winter day when I was very little and very cold I crawled under the cloth, and it was wonderfully warm, so I curled up like a kitten to take a nap. They looked for me everywhere and couldn't find me." She chuckled at the thought, then added ruefully, "Meanwhile, I was almost asphyxiated, of course."

"It all sounds so different," Dick mused. "I'd love to see Japan."

"You must come!" Jenny said, sure of a welcome for her American cousin. "You must come and stay with us."

Dick threw back his head and laughed heartily. "I'll skip over for a September weekend," he promised. "That is, if you'll be home."

"Oh, I'll be home," retorted Jenny. Then she thought, My goodness, I will be!

She glanced at her grandmother, but found she wasn't listening. Mrs. Smith was standing looking out of the windows, which opened on the water. In the distance a pair of white sailboats were skimming along on the breeze, and closer at hand a water skier was weaving in an intricate pattern at the end of a line attached to a motorboat. "It's beautiful," she said.

And so peaceful, Jenny might have replied. It was the peacefulness that impressed her most. Accustomed to crowded Tokyo, Kansas City had seemed spacious,

149

but Cape Cod had still another quality, a sweeping vista of earth and water and sky, which made her soul feel rested and refreshed.

Jenny tried to explain in a letter to Yukari. She wrote:

> We have moved to a summer resort on Cape Cod, a small peninsula, shaped like an arm bending right-angled. We're staying at an inn on the tip of the elbow, facing a beautiful bay.
>
> The color of the water changes according to the time of day, almost white in the morning, radiant blue in the afternoon, and gray in the evening. Peeping through the curtain of my bedside window at dawn, I see white fishing boats going out to the Atlantic Ocean leaving a feather of surf behind. When the first star appears they come back, loaded with their catch and followed by hundreds of sea gulls, swarming to get the fish heads the men heave overboard.
>
> Today, while my grandmother played golf and my cousin Dick went sailing with a school friend, I went down to the beach and lay in the sun. Almost nobody was around, and it seemed like my own beach even though it belongs to the inn. Can you imagine such privacy? I remember when you and I went to Enoshima Beach and struggled to find water among people.

Unconsciously, in her final sentence, Jenny Kimura had reverted to the Japanese habit of eliminating articles. She thought in two languages with equal ease, but sometimes the mannerisms of one crept into the other quite innocently. In personality also Jenny was becoming more ambivalent. Sometimes these days she felt more American than Japanese, although in Tokyo she had been rooted firmly to her mother's culture.

If it hadn't been for her longing to see Alan, Jenny would have enjoyed thoroughly the relaxed atmosphere of the sunny summer days at the Cape. There was enough to do, but not too much, and she had time to get to know her cousin better.

Sometimes Dick acted like a brother, at other times like a beau. He took Jenny bicycling, escorted her to the summer theater, and lay with her for long hours on the beach, just talking, while gulls wheeled overhead and sandpipers skittered along at the water's edge. He was neither as carefree nor as animated as Alan Carlisle, but Jenny began to feel that Dick was a person of considerable depth. He had firm intentions about his future—like his stepfather, he wanted to teach—and he also felt a deep responsibility for his grandmother, which Jenny didn't quite understand.

She questioned him about it one morning when he seemed especially restless. "Have you enjoyed coming here, summer after summer?"

"Not really. I get a lot of reading done, but I feel useless, as though I should be working," Dick admitted. "If Grandy weren't so alone!" He always called his grandmother by this affectionate diminutive, and he acted protective toward her, teasing her, flattering her, and treating her more like a child than like a person three times his age. "Next year I want to go abroad," he continued after a minute, "but I scarcely know how to tell her. Since my grandfather died, I'm the only one she has left."

"*Our* grandfather," Jenny corrected gently. "I've seen his picture. He looks as though he must have been a wonderfully vigorous old man."

"Oh, he was!" Dick said. "And he wasn't half as pigheaded as Grandy—about your father, I mean. Of course, he died when I was only Laurie's age, but I remember his patting me on the shoulder and saying, 'We must give your grandmother time, boy, but she'll come around.'"

"I wonder," Jenny murmured. "I suppose inviting me here was a great concession. She still seems embarrassed sometimes when people look at me curiously in the dining room."

"They're interested, not critical," Dick growled. "Anyway, Grandy has taken one big step forward, and, who knows, maybe she'll take another someday."

"Be friendly with Daddy, you mean?"

Dick nodded. "What's he like, Jenny? Do you suppose he's anything like—like—"

"Like his brother?" Jenny finished. "I don't know. He's big and nice and sort of noisy, but gentle too. And he likes doing things with his hands."

"I was born after my father left for the Pacific," Dick said, turning over on his stomach and idly running sand through his fingers. "He never even saw me. I guess it was pretty tough for Mom, as well as for my—*our*—grandmother."

Jenny nodded. "There must have been so many tragedies in those days."

"I suppose if he'd been killed in anything but hand-to-hand combat, if he'd been blown up in a plane or drowned at sea or anything else at all, she might not have been so bitter. But as it was, when your father married a Jap, Grandy really took it hard."

Jenny stiffened, finding the use of the word *Jap* as distasteful as though her cousin had called a Negro a nigger. "My Japanese grandparents were also very unhappy that my mother married an American," she said with asperity.

"They were? Why?"

"They are landowners," Jenny replied. "In their village they are looked down upon because they have an American son-in-law. They wouldn't attend the wedding, and my parents have never had a single meal in my Japanese grandparents' house."

"For Pete's sake!" breathed Dick, in such amazement that Jenny could tell this was an idea so strange that it was utterly baffling.

"It makes my mother very sad," Jenny continued. "Once a year on New Year's Day we always go to the village to pay our respects, and when we leave, Mother always cries a little, because her parents remain so stern and unyielding, even after all these years."

Dick was frowning in concentration. "I still don't understand," he admitted. "Was it—Hiroshima?"

"Oh no," replied Jenny at once. "It has nothing to

153

do with the war. It's just that my mother was an only daughter, and it would have been proper for her to marry a man of good family, not a foreigner, don't you see?"

"What's wrong with the Smiths?" Dick asked so pugnaciously that Jenny burst out laughing.

"Suppose I asked Grandmother, 'What's wrong with the Kimuras?' There isn't any answer to a question like that."

Dick gave a long sigh and scratched his head ruefully. "It beats me," he said. "It really does." Then, as though he was tired of wasting time on an insoluble problem, he got to his feet and suggested abruptly, "Come on, let's go for a swim."

There were other conversations between Jenny Kimura and her cousin that cemented their growing understanding of one another. Jenny discovered that Dick was not only tender-hearted and intensely curious. He was also filled with admiration for learning and serious about his college career. "I'm not terribly bright," he said honestly. "I mean I'm not a quick study or anything. My grades are just average. But I want to work in education. I think the most important thing a person can do is to help other people broaden their knowledge. I could never be just another businessman."

"What do you want to teach?" Jenny asked.

"I *think* history or philosophy, but I'm not really sure," Dick replied frankly. "It worries me, sort of."

"That's what Alan Carlisle said."

154

"Alan Carlisle? Who's he?"

"A boy I met in Kansas City," explained Jenny. "He's going to a college named Williams, and he doesn't know what he wants to be, either. The only difference is, he doesn't know *at all*."

"The kids who are *sure* are the lucky ones," Dick grumbled. "You've got to get started early these days." Then he shifted the subject slightly. "I heard Mother talking to you about coming back to the States for college. You ought to consider it seriously, Jenny. Then you could spend holidays with Grandy. She *needs* you, actually."

But Jenny shook her head. "I think Grandmother is very self-sufficient. I don't thinks she needs anyone."

"That's where you're wrong," objected Dick immediately. "She just gives that impression. At heart Grandy's an old softie, and if she could only bring herself to it, a reunion with your dad would be the greatest thing ever. Because she needs him too."

Need. It was a word that Jenny would never have associated with her grandmother. Thinking about it later, she tried to imagine what urgent want could not be satisfied, and only then did she fully realize Dick's meaning. Her grandmother needed the love of her family—of her own son and her two grandchildren. She had Dick's affection, certainly, but one out of three was not enough.

And while Jenny had been courteous and considerate, had she really been loving this summer? She had been appreciative, she had tried to be understanding, but except for one occasion, which had rather disturbed her afterward, had she ever been spontaneously affectionate?

Jenny was walking along the beach at the tide's edge, pondering this question and occasionally stooping to pick up a miniature starfish or an interesting shell, when she saw, coming toward her, a young man who was conspicuously Japanese. His hair was black and straight, his skin burnished, his eyes tilted at the corners. There was no question of his parentage. He might have stepped straight off a suburban train in Tokyo.

As he drew closer, however, Jenny realized that he was taller than average, huskier, with a glow of health, which showed in his erect carriage and swinging stride. As he drew closer he looked as startled as Jenny. "Hi!" he said, pulling up short. "Where did you drop from? Or am I seeing things?"

Jenny smiled. "I'm staying at the inn." She indicated with a glance the wooden steps climbing the wall of the bluff.

"Good! So am I," said this astonishing stranger, who spoke English without a trace of accent. "We just arrived today."

"Dóko kará kimáshita ka?" asked Jenny, involuntarily falling into Japanese.

The young man looked puzzled, then burst out laughing in a manner that reminded Jenny of Alan's spontaneity. "Sorry," he said. "You'll have to translate. I don't speak Japanese."

"You don't?" Jenny stopped short and looked skeptical. Surely he was teasing.

"No kidding," came the quick answer. "I'm a Californian. I've never been to Japan."

Naturally Jenny had heard of nisei, Japanese born in America, but this was her first encounter with one, and she waited while he introduced himself. "My name is George Yamada, and I'm working here as a tutor for a family named Selden, who seem to think I can work a miracle and get their two kids through high-school math."

"I'm Jenny Kimura—Jenny Kimura Smith."

"Aha! That explains it. You're only half Japanese."

Jenny nodded, smiling shyly.

"You work here too?"

"No, I'm staying with my grandmother," Jenny replied briefly. She was beginning to wonder whether this casual meeting would be considered the proper basis for an acquaintanceship.

George seemed to understand, because he grinned and said, "Don't be nervous. You won't be scolded for talking to me. Actually, if you like, I can get myself introduced."

"I think that would be very nice," murmured Jenny, relieved. Then she cried delightedly, "Oh, it's fun to find somebody who looks like people you've always known!"

At this George Yamada seemed more amused than ever. "But I'm not, you know," he warned her. "I'm strictly American—second generation, in fact." He would have continued, but was interrupted by a shout from the steps. Two skinny teen-agers came racing down to the beach carrying water skis and signaling to George.

"See you later," said Jenny's new friend. "That's Pat and Peter. Duty calls."

❦ TWELVE

That evening after dinner Mr. and Mrs. Selden, who had known Jenny's grandmother from previous summers, introduced their children's tutor in the friendliest way imaginable. They brought him over to Mrs. Smith's table and invited Jenny and Dick to join them on a beach picnic the next day.

"We've chartered a small boat for water-skiing and traveling to and from the outer bar and Monomoy," said Mr. Selden. "George, here, runs it like an old hand, so you need have no qualms."

Jenny's eyes sparkled with excitement. She had been anxious to see the other side of the long sand strip, visible across half a mile of open water, but the opportunity had not presented itself. Now Mrs. Smith seemed strangely reluctant to give her permission. "Wasn't it tomorrow," she asked Dick, "that you were planning to drive Jenny to Provincetown?"

Jenny watched her cousin, who seemed to be ignoring some message discernible in his grandmother's eyes. "Provincetown will keep," he said blithely. "I think a beach picnic sounds dandy. Jenny, how about you?"

"I'd love it!" Jenny spoke enthusiastically, and the Seldens must have counted this an acceptance, because they nodded and turned back to Mrs. Smith. "You'll come too?"

"Thank you, but I'm playing golf," said Jenny's grandmother, who still seemed concerned about something. She glanced from Dick to George Yamada appraisingly, but raised no further objection, and arrangements were made for the young people to meet on the beach at noon.

When Jenny and Dick came down the steps from the bluff at the appointed time the next day, they discovered that two boats were pulled up on the sand. The second one belonged to another family staying at the inn, people of Norwegian descent who were positively Viking in their blond good looks. The Hansens had a fourteen-year-old daughter named Christina, who had brought along a friend about the age of the Selden boys, Anne Watson, and at the last minute another girl had been invited—Eileen King, a beautiful creature with silky brown hair and Irish blue eyes, who looked as innocent as a kitten and who managed to appear just about as helpless, quickly captivating Dick.

There was the usual hubbub accompanying the loading and launching, but finally the two boats, their outboards roaring, scuttled off like beetles across the water, and Jenny, hemmed in between a huge picnic hamper and Mrs. Selden, breathed deeply as her hair blew straight out in the quickening breeze.

For her the ride seemed far too short. She could have stayed in the boat for an hour, thrilling to the sense of speed, the smell of salt, the foaming white wake, and the sun's caress. But within ten minutes the men were anchoring the small craft on the opposite shore, and everyone was piling out into the shallow water, laden with hampers, towels, rugs, and cartons of soft drinks.

George Yamada helped Mr. Selden secure the boat fore and aft, then caught up with Jenny as she trudged with the others along a ragged path through the beach grass, which blew silver then green as the breeze shifted. Dunes lay ahead and the ocean was invisible, but Jenny was filled with anticipation of a new experience. If George had only been Alan Carlisle it would have been an altogether perfect day!

However, there was no genie at hand to work such alchemy, and it would have been foolish not to make the best of the available companionship. She smiled at George warmly, accepted his offer of help with her burden, and stepped aside so that Pat and Peter Selden could scamper ahead like irrepressible puppies, anxious to be the first ones to scale the dunes.

As it happened, Jenny Kimura and George arrived last. They stood for some minutes on the rise from which they could first glimpse the boundless ocean and the long broad beach, while Jenny breathed, "Oh, isn't it beautiful! Isn't it vast!" To the south, down the line of dunes, there was nothing to be seen but a wheeling tern and a shelf of sand washed by white-capped combers. The surf's roar was continuous, drowning the voices of the picnic party, but it soothed Jenny rather than disturbed her, and she loved the emptiness of the miles of beach.

To the north, so far away that they looked like toy soldiers, two fishermen were standing knee-deep in the water, and behind them, in the shelter of the dunes, stood a dilapidated truck.

"Beach buggy," said George.

"Buggy?" Jenny looked down at her bare legs but could discover no flies or mosquitoes. "I don't think so. At least they're not biting me."

George let out an amused guffaw, then pointed at the truck. "Not bugs," he explained. "Buggy. That's what the fishermen call the heaps they rig up for camping trips, with oversized tires and cookstoves and cots and things."

"Oh," Jenny murmured, abashed by her own naïveté. She was even more disconcerted when George slid down the dune to regale the rest of the party with news of her mistake. She hung back, rather daunted, but found that the slip seemed to endear her to the adults and young people alike. They were amused, but they were also delighted that she had made such a natural error, and Jenny felt as though a gate had opened. They no longer treated her like an outsider, but welcomed her into their midst.

Jenny made herself useful. While the boys gathered wood for a fire, she helped Mrs. Selden spread rugs, unpack the picnic hampers, and arrange a big plate of fresh fruit. The other young people by now had raced into the surf, squealing at the shock of the icy water, but Jenny lingered behind until her hostess shooed her away.

Not for anything would she have admitted that the waves frightened her, because Dick and George were both having great sport riding the combers into the beach. Eileen, swimming with her hair clinging to her head and looking like a seal, joined them, but Jenny stood knee-deep in the surf, unable to bring herself to dive through the first rough waves and reach the calm water beyond. It was her first experience with undertow, and she felt that if she slipped into one of the receding troughs she would be pulled to the very bottom of the sea. But, instead of acknowledging her fear, she pretended to Dick and George that she found the water too cold. "Maybe after lunch," she said, stalling for time.

After lunch, however, Mrs. Selden insisted that the young people wait for an hour before swimming again. So, while the adults strolled up the beach toward the persistent surf fishermen, the young people prepared to amuse themselves in various ways. Dick and Eileen went back to some tidal pools beyond the dunes, searching for tern nests. Dick said that at this time of year the young were to be found in the sand, fluffy as Easter-basket ducklings, and Eileen was anxious to see the baby birds. The Selden boys, along with Anne and Christina, straggled after them, but Jenny couldn't bring herself to leave the beach.

"I think I'll walk toward the point," she said to the others, wanting to be alone, to see whether the song of the sea accounted for her exciting and pleasant sense of expectancy.

But George said, "Mind if I come along?" and fell into step beside her on the damp, hard sand.

They walked silently for a few minutes, while the sun beat down on their bare heads and a few brown herring gulls circled above the blowing beach grass on the dunes. The sand at their feet was ornamented with shells and polished pebbles, gifts of the sea, and pricked with the tracks of sandpipers, who scurried ahead as Jenny and George approached. In spite of the roar of the turbulent ocean there was, about this outer bar, a sense of pure peace.

After a while Jenny said, "I wish you knew Japan. You'd understand why I find this—this emptiness—so remarkable. There's no place like it in our islands— at least nothing that I've ever seen. Why, even Mount Fuji, on a clear summer day like this, is positively teeming with climbers, going up, coming down, picnicking, camping. But here!" Jenny spread her arms, as though she wanted to embrace the solitude.

George looked at her sympathetically, but what he said was surprising. "You're so different from American girls."

"I am? Why?"

"I don't know. Maybe it's because you think differently."

"At home my friends say I'm very American," Jenny said. Then, because she felt it ill-mannered to talk

164

about herself, she said, "You are even more surprising, George. You look Japanese, but you act American."

"Why wouldn't I? I *am* an American. I was born here and so were my parents. Even my grandparents lived here until they were old."

"Tell me about your ancestors. Where did they come from?"

"A place called Nara. Do you know it?"

Jenny nodded. "There's a wonderful deer park there, and the Daibutsu, a great black Buddha kept in the largest wooden building in Japan."

"My grandparents," George continued, "had a farm in California and grew apricots. That's all I know about them, really. When they had saved enough money they went back and died in Nara, but my father stayed on."

"Is he a farmer, too?"

George's eyes clouded. "He was, before the war. You know what happened to the Japanese in California, of course?"

Jenny tried to remember her smattering of American history. "They were put in camps or something?"

"Segregation centers. I guess it was natural for the government to be frightened, but my parents were American citizens. They were as loyal as—as the President himself!"

"I'm sure they were," murmured Jenny comfortingly, but wondered why it seemed to matter to George so desperately. The war was long past, and he hadn't even been born then—or had he? "When were you born?" she asked.

165

"In 1944," George answered, as though the year were significant. "At Tule Lake, behind barbed wire. There were 18,000 Japanese Americans there, a good many of them coming, as my parents did, from the assembly center at the Santa Anita racetrack. It must have been a terrible time. They were all so grief-stricken and lost."

"Grief-stricken?" Jenny Kimura repeated questioningly.

George nodded. "They had their little farms, their houses and furniture. When the evacuation orders came in the early summer of 1941, they were in the worst bargaining position possible. They had to clear out after planting time and before the harvest. Because they had the same ancestors as the Japanese enemy, they were forced to sell everything they owned at distressed prices. They were truly dispossessed."

"How terrible," Jenny murmured. "I never knew—"

George suddenly straightened, as though he realized he mustn't spoil this beautiful day with a tale of disaster. "Of course, there's a bright side too," he said more cheerfully. "My father says that our people turned the tragedy of evacuation into a display of loyalty. Very few renounced their citizenship. Many thousands came out from the camps as my parents did, still believing in the essential goodness of America, and willing to start over again."

Turning at last to start back toward the picnic spot, George seemed very real and vivid and close at hand. In an hour's time Jenny had come to know him better than she knew her own cousin and—yes!—far better than she knew Alan Carlisle. She had come into contact with another sensitive human being, who shared her own feeling of disorientation, but for quite a different reason. She felt as though they were kindred spirits, as though their minds and feelings had touched.

George Yamada was not the person he appeared to be on the surface. He was American in his attitudes, which was natural. This was the environment into which he had been born. But he still had the acuteness of feeling as well as the appearance of his Japanese ancestors. Great sensibility should be treated with gentleness, and this gentleness Jenny knew she possessed.

"Do you ever feel you want to talk to a person who doesn't exist?" George asked her. "Someone completely understanding?" He stopped and seized Jenny's hand, crushing it roughly in an excess of emotion. "I feel as if that person is you."

Jenny didn't answer. If George felt that she was this nebulous confidante of his dreams, she mustn't destroy the illusion, although she wished he were a little less intense. She wished he were simply fun-loving, gay, and charming, like Alan Carlisle. To have walked on this beach with Alan—that would have been heaven indeed. What was George saying now? That he liked her—"I like you because you're so mysterious."

Jenny tried to oblige by smiling mysteriously, but she felt like a traitor, because she had been concerned with thoughts of another boy. "I like you too," she said, in an effort to atone.

This was a mistake. It encouraged George to the point of giddiness, and for the rest of the afternoon he followed Jenny like a shadow. "What are you doing tonight?" he asked, and when she made some excuse he persisted. "Tomorrow night? Let's go to the movies, or to the band concert in the square."

"With Dick?" Jenny asked, but George shook his head. "Dick can find himself a girl. Three's a crowd."

Mrs. Smith was extremely reluctant when Jenny asked permission to go out the next evening with George Yamada. "He's too old for you, Jenny. He's nineteen or twenty, at least."

At this Dick unexpectedly came to his cousin's rescue. "He's *just* nineteen, Grandy, and he's a swell kid."

"Will you be along?" his grandmother asked.

Dick shook his head. "I'm going out with Eileen King." Then he grinned disarmingly. "After all, Jenny and I are first cousins. You wouldn't want us to go steady, would you now?"

"Don't be ridiculous!" Mrs. Smith snorted. "Who said anything about such a thing? But I can't see why any stray Japanese who comes along should act as though Jenny were his for the picking. What do we know about this boy?"

"For one thing, we know he's American," said Jenny. Although it hadn't mattered much up until now, suddenly she was determined to have a date with George.

"Don't be stuffy, Grandy," Dick was saying. "Jenny's got to get around a little. I bet when you were sixteen you had lots of beaus!"

As always, such teasing softened Mrs. Smith's attitude. "Go on with you!" she said to Dick, but then she gave in with a shrug. "All right, Jennifer, but be back at the inn no later than eleven. And take a sweater. It turns cold here at night."

THIRTEEN

Jenny enjoyed going out with George Yamada. The evening at the band concert was dreamy and restful, a page straight out of the past. In a hexagonal bandstand scarlet-coated musicians played marches and popular tunes, while summer people and native Cape Codders sat on blankets and coats on the grass. There were balloons and fireflies and a sky full of stars. There was a picture-book quality about the scene that Jenny loved, and she was sure she would never forget the bright colors of the children's clothes, the velvet sky, and the feeling that she had stepped back in time to her grandmother's day.

Afterward George and Jenny walked back to the inn by way of the beach, moving into a path of moonlight as they left the laughter and music behind. Jenny kicked off her shoes and carried them in her hand, listening to George talk about his ambition to be an architect—a really *great* architect, like Le Corbusier or

Wright or Belluschi. He was hoping to take his graduate work at M.I.T., he said, right in Boston, where he could work under some of the best teachers in the United States.

Compared to Alan, George seemed mature to Jenny, very dedicated, very much a man. She was flattered by his interest in her and was glad to listen to his plans for the future. It was like taking wing to walk in the moonpath beside him. She felt as though they could leap up and soar like a pair of gulls, if they only tried.

The sense of sharing another person's excitement was new to Jenny, and pleasurable. When George asked her to go to the summer theater two nights hence, Jenny accepted, knowing that she would have Dick's support in persuading her grandmother. Over the weekend George took her to the movies, and early the following week he and Dick taught her to water-ski.

Jenny was well-coordinated. She got up on the skis on her second try and found that she could ride the salt water with a lightness and ease that filled her with delight. Once she learned the trick of balance she was confident, and before the week was out she had acquired the technique of planing, so that she could ski far out from the boat, leaving a white wake of her own making.

Now whenever the young tutor wasn't occupied with the Selden boys, he sought Jenny out. The pair swam and sunned and talked together by the hour, becoming so companionable that Mrs. Smith criticized Jenny pointedly.

171

"Is it because George looks so Japanese that Grandmother doesn't like him?" Jenny asked Dick in private.

"Could be. But you forget you insisted to Grandy that he's American!" Dick's eyes twinkled. "What I can't understand," he added, "is what George sees in *you*."

Jenny had become inured to her cousin's teasing and could give as good as she got. "He says I'm mysterious," she said with a sly glance.

"Mysterious?" Dick hooted in derision. "You're about as mysterious as cellophane!"

"Why, Dick! I thought we were friends."

"We are. But mysterious! For Pete's sake, George should be able to see right through you. I know what you're interested in, boys and clothes, in that order, just like any other girl."

This pleased Jenny, instead of annoying her. Dick's raillery always made her feel cherished and secure. Besides, she realized that in George she had acquired a devoted swain. No longer did she sit on the sidelines, dependent upon her cousin or her grandmother to take her places. Jenny was having still another new experience. She was discovering the enjoyment of being adored.

Then, one day in the afternoon mail, came a letter from Alan Carlisle. The envelope carried a hodgepodge of forwarding addresses, but finally, after three weeks, it had at last caught up with her. She was alone when she found it on the mail desk, but even so Jenny didn't open the letter at once. She needed particular privacy, such as she couldn't find in the cottage or on the beach at this time of day, so she ran across the lawn to a grove of trees, which had been left as a screen between the inn and the next property, and found a sheltered spot behind a clump of high-bush blueberries. Then, with trembling fingers, she tore at the envelope's flap. Alan had written:

Dear Jenny,
I haven't heard a word from you! Didn't I give you my address? Just c/o Roger Gibson will get me. Bass River, Cape Cod, Mass.

Jenny could scarcely believe her eyes. Alan was here, here on Cape Cod! It was incredible. It was wonderful! Why, he might be within a few miles of this very spot. He might even come to see her! Jenny's eyes grew moist with emotion and her heart leaped.

The rest of the letter seemed unimportant, but she was glad to know Alan missed her. He'd call her the minute he got back to Kansas City. "Let Mother rave, if she likes!" he said, then added that he was brown as an Indian, but not having a very good time. "The girls around here are all sappy. They giggle at everything."

Even this news was good, almost too good to be true. Jenny clasped the letter to her breast and rocked back and forth happily, then jumped up and raced back across the lawn to the inn, where a Cape Cod map hung in the lounge.

It took her quite a while to find Bass River, which was a thin uneven line running across the Cape from the south shore. It wasn't near, but it wasn't terribly far away, perhaps twenty-five or thirty miles. There was a village by the same name, a black dot on Route 28. Not an impossible distance from the inn if Alan could borrow his mother's car.

But of course he couldn't. At least, not if his mother knew that he would be coming to see me, Jenny thought. This opened up a maze of problems. How could she get in touch with him without his mother's becoming suspicious? Mrs. Carlisle already knew Jenny's handwriting, because naturally she had written a note of thanks for the dinner. A ruse occurred to her. She might get Dick to address the envelope!

This entailed a confession. "You remember I told you about a boy in Kansas City named Alan Carlisle?" Jenny asked her cousin at the first opportunity.

"Vaguely."

"Well, he's here on the Cape," Jenny said. "At a place called Bass River." She was unaware that she was twisting her hands nervously.

But Dick noticed, and raised his head, sniffing. "Do I scent romance?"

Jenny flushed and bit her lip. This afternoon she had no time for teasing. "I want to write him a note," she said, "but his mother doesn't like me. Will you do me a favor and address the envelope?"

At this Dick put down the fishing rod he was rigging and looked at Jenny as though such a request staggered belief. "Why, you little schemer!" he marveled. "Just like that you invite me to be an accessory after the fact."

174

"Oh, no!" Jenny objected. "I want you for an accomplice." She put out a hand and touched her cousin's arm. "Please, Dick."

"Oh, sure. For you I'd do anything," Dick replied. "But don't blame me if you get into trouble. Imagine, Jenny Kimura Smith chasing a boy!"

"I'm not chasing him!" Jenny retorted, quite horrified, then realized that Dick was still teasing, and broke off.

"Why doesn't his mother like you?" her cousin asked more seriously.

"For the same reason Grandmother doesn't like George Yamada, I guess."

Dick gave a long, expressive whistle. "Well, you certainly don't mince words, Jenny."

"It's the truth, isn't it?"

Dick didn't reply.

"Isn't it?" Jenny pressed.

Finally Dick nodded. "But remember, honey, Grandy and her friends are from another generation. Our crowd will see things differently."

This was scant comfort. Jenny was concerned with the here and now, and with every passing second her desire to see Alan increased. She walked all the way to the village post office with the letter, so it would go out by the first possible mail, and only resisted adding a special-delivery stamp because she didn't want the note to attract undue attention in Alan's uncle's house.

"This will reach Bass River tomorrow?" she asked

the postal clerk anxiously, as she gave her treasured communication into his personal care.

"You bet," the man promised, smiling at Jenny's earnestness. "Tomorrow first thing!"

The next morning, after Mrs. Smith left for her thrice-weekly golf game, Jenny stayed in the cottage within reach of the telephone. She washed her hair and toweled it dry, brushing it until it shone. Then she manicured her nails, plucked a few stray hairs from her eyebrows, and inspected her face in the mirror more critically than she had since leaving home.

One thing pleased her. She'd slimmed down again. Between swimming, bicycling, and water-skiing, a sport at which she was becoming adept, she was getting plenty of exercise. But her skin was the color of brown sugar, and this dismayed her. She must wear a sun hat and a beach coat whenever she could.

Japanese girls admired pale skins, and Jenny shared this taste. When Dick said, "Boy, you've got a gorgeous suntan," she couldn't believe he meant it, because she would have preferred to be as blond as Christina Hansen, had she been given her choice. Yet, when she tried to imagine herself with pale yellow hair, it was too ridiculous. She wasn't a chameleon; she was a black-haired, quite Oriental-looking girl.

And apparently Alan had liked her just as she was. Pacing up and down the room, Jenny wondered whether the postman had delivered her letter, whether the phone would ring in the next few minutes, or whether the suspense would last until this afternoon.

Lunchtime arrived. Mrs. Smith was staying on to

play bridge at the club, and Dick had gone sailing again with his school friend, so in spite of hunger pangs Jenny decided she would skip the meal. Suppose the telephone call came when she was out.

At two o'clock there was a knock on the door, and Jenny answered it in a flurry. But it was George Yamada who stood there, a pair of water skis over his shoulder and an invitation on his lips. "Come on down to the beach and—"

Already Jenny was shaking her head. "I can't—today," she interrupted. "I've got to stay here. I'm expecting a telephone call."

George looked concerned. "Something wrong at home?"

"No," Jenny confessed, but she didn't elaborate.

George let the skis slide to the ground and leaned on them. "I don't have to go now. I could wait."

"Oh no! No thank you," Jenny said quickly. "You go on. I've got some things I really must do, if you'll excuse me." She was appalled at the thought that the phone might ring while George stood there, listening in. But after the door was shut she was sorry that she had sounded so sharp. George was a dear, kind and understanding and devoted, a really good friend.

Nevertheless, he wasn't Alan. The picture of Alan that Jenny carried in her mind was larger than life size perhaps, but it was also very appealing. She could hardly wait to see him and hear his voice. Again she paced, then rummaged through an abandoned picnic basket and found some stale crackers to nibble on. Three o'clock came and went, and the hands of the clock began to move closer and closer to four. A car door slammed and her grandmother came in. Tossing a sweater on the sofa, she said, "Good heavens, child, why aren't you out in the sunshine on this beautiful day?"

"I was washing my hair." Jenny offered the first excuse she could think of.

"In the middle of the afternoon? How silly. You ought to be on the beach."

Just like a grown-up! Jenny thought. The beach or the tennis court was the panacea for all ills. If one was busy, one was automatically cheerful and happy. Idleness was unthinkable.

"I'm going to take a bath," Mrs. Smith announced, as though this were of equal importance to Jenny's well-being. She was already unbuttoning her golf shirt as she walked across to her bedroom door. "Was there any mail?"

Jenny couldn't admit she hadn't been to the dining room for lunch. "I didn't look," she murmured.

"Well, go over and see, will you, sweetie?" suggested Mrs. Smith calmly, as she disappeared from sight.

There was nothing to do but acquiesce. Jenny ran to the inn and ran back again, her heart pumping. "Just one or two bills," she called across the rush of water from the bathroom tap. Then she resumed her vigil, hiding behind the pages of one of the books she had borrowed from the Harringtons. When it was time, she changed for dinner, but she did so listlessly. It was easy to make excuses for Alan. He could be

178

away for the day; he could have gone to Province-town or even to Boston. Nevertheless, Jenny was shattered that he hadn't yet called.

Throughout the evening meal she was unusually quiet, picking at the steak which Dick considered a treat but which Jenny found almost repulsive. She didn't share the American appetite for rare, thick beef, even though she found most of the food (especially ice cream) superb. "If you don't want that I'll eat it," Dick suggested, and she passed her plate over to her cousin quite willingly.

"Don't you feel well, Jenny?" Mrs. Smith put out a hand and touched her granddaughter's forehead. "D'you think you have a temperature?"

Jenny shook her head, and was about to protest, "I'm quite all right," when one of the college girls who acted as waitresses came up to the table and said, "Jenny, there's a telephone call for you."

"Oh, thank you." Mumbling an "Excuse me" to her grandmother, Jenny pushed back her chair so abruptly it almost turned over. She hurried across the dining room, weaving between the tables, and almost collided with some incoming guests as she scampered through the lobby to the booth at the end of the hall.

"Hello." Even to her own ears Jenny's voice sounded weak and faint.

"Jenny Kimura? Hi, it's Alan Carlisle."

"I know. How are you?" What a mundane, insipid thing to say, Jenny thought, but how could you tell a boy the very sound of his voice made you want to shout and sing?

179

"Swell! It sure was a surprise to get your letter."

"It was a surprise to get yours, too. I didn't know Bass River was on the Cape."

"Are you having a good summer?" Alan asked.

"Yes," Jenny said a trifle hesitantly. "Are you?"

"So-so. I told you in my letter, didn't I?"

Jenny forced herself to be bold. "Do you think you could come to see me?" she asked in a faint and breathless voice.

"I'd sure like to, but there are complications. Such as a car, I mean."

"There's a bus," Jenny said instantly. She had checked schedules in the village yesterday afternoon when she'd gone to mail the letter. "It runs every two hours."

"Buses, ugh," muttered Alan disparagingly. Then he asked, "What are you doing next Tuesday? Mother's going to Duxbury with Aunt Helen. Maybe I could get the car."

Monday, Tuesday, any day would have been fine with Jenny! This was no time for subterfuge. She cried, "Wonderful! Will you come for lunch?"

"Sure, if you ask me," Alan said.

"Come as early as you can," suggested Jenny persuasively. "And bring your swimming trunks."

"Your time is up," the operator's voice cut in. "Please signal when through."

"Good-bye," Alan called, and "Good-bye," Jenny replied. She put the receiver back in its cradle and leaned weakly against the closed door of the booth while the sound of Alan's voice still echoed in her ears. Tuesday. She would see him Tuesday! A wave of excitement made her tremble. Alan—here!

When Jenny returned to the dining room her head was high. "That was Alan Carlisle calling," she told her grandmother at once. "He's staying with some relatives in Bass River, and I've asked him over for lunch next Tuesday. I hope you don't mind."

"Hmph," said Mrs. Smith, as though no further comment was needed. She didn't look displeased, although she raised her eyebrows. Then, moving her coffee cup ever so slightly away from her, she sat back and regarded Jenny Kimura with an amused and admiring smile.

🌺 FOURTEEN

Tuesday wasn't especially slow in coming, for the very good reason that George Yamada helped Jenny fill her spare time. She didn't tell him about Alan, partly from shyness, partly from fear that she might hurt his feelings if she confessed interest in another boy. Meanwhile, she cherished the astonishing realization that she was being sought after by two young men at the same time. Imagine Yukari's envy, Jenny thought, if she could be with me now!

Such attention was enough to increase any girl's confidence, and Jenny Kimura was no exception to the rule. She walked with a lighter step, laughed at the slightest provocation, and allowed her American heritage to gain ascendancy over her Japanese upbringing. With Jenny's grandmother and cousin her position started to undergo a subtle change. They seemed to like her new display of spirit, and she felt that Alan's continued interest was giving her a certain status in their eyes.

Deliberately, Jenny pushed to the back of her mind the one thing that troubled her. It was obvious from their telephone conversation that Alan had not told his mother that he was planning to spend a day with her. I won't see him again, Jenny promised herself virtuously, until this thing is straightened out between them. I won't have him sneaking off to see me as though I were a disreputable character.

But just this once. . . .

Such a bold, unaccustomed, and daring decision to have made, all on her own! It occurred to Jenny that her mother would have been horrified at her change in personality, as she also would have been at the idea of her sixteen-year-old daughter's going out—alone!—with two different young men. But customs were different here, Japan was far away, and Jenny decided that her grandmother's approval was all she need worry about.

Life was suddenly becoming very exciting, as though her dreams of America were about to come true. Jenny felt like the heroine of a novel, and had to remind herself that she must continue to appear demure and polite when she felt like shouting. Oh, it was a wonderful thing to be alive!

This sense of buoyancy carried Jenny right through to the moment when Alan appeared, shortly after eleven o'clock on Tuesday morning, coming across the lawn with his jaunty stride, to pull up short in front of the screen door.

"Hi," he said, grinning.

"Hello, Alan." For a moment Jenny was afraid that her voice must sound as husky as her Aunt Virginia's. Then she smiled and held out her hand, flinching only slightly at the hardness of Alan's grip. "You *are* tan!"

"Boy, so are you!" Alan replied, as Jenny stepped out into the sunlight. He looked at her appraisingly, as though he were seeing her afresh.

"This seashore sun—" Jenny faltered, then was rescued by Dick, who came out of the door behind her, ready to be introduced.

The two boys greeted each other casually, acting as though there was no need for treating this visit as a special occasion. Jenny, accustomed to the ceremonial bowing and tea drinking that always welcomed a visitor to her home in Tokyo, still found such lack of manners disconcerting, but had learned to show no surprise.

The trio went into the cottage living room, where Mrs. Smith was gathering up her sunglasses and purse, getting ready to go off to an antique auction with a friend. "If I'm not back by one o'clock, go on and have lunch without me," she suggested, after she had said a few words of greeting to Alan. "Jenny, you can be hostess in my place."

It was all part of the same pattern, Jenny thought, one that all Americans accepted, but which she still found difficult to understand. She nodded, said, "Have a good time, Grandmother," and returned her attention to the boys, who were leaning together over a card table upon which Dick had spread an assortment of maps. He had been trying to plot Napoleon's retreat from Waterloo, and enlisted Alan's aid, offering his opinion of the faults in the Emperor's strategy and suggesting that *he* would have managed things better, had he been in command.

Alan got interested in the tactical problems, and, to Jenny's growing confusion, he quite ignored her. Finally she said, "When you boys are ready, let's go for a swim."

She went into her bedroom and changed, coming back with a cap and a towel, but Alan and Dick were still engaged in Napoleonic maneuvers, and in an effort to break up the conference she pretended indignation, saying, "I'll see you down on the beach." Crossing the lawn to the bluff, she walked slowly, and going down the steps she positively dawdled, hoping that Alan would catch up with her, but minutes passed and she arrived on the sand alone.

George Yamada was there before her. On most mornings he was engaged with lessons, but today he hurried across the sand with some unexpected news. "Guess what! The Seldens have all gone off with some friends on a schooner. I've got a holiday!"

Jenny was a trifle dismayed. "How nice," she murmured. Then she couldn't resist asking, "Why didn't you go too?"

"Me? I'm just hired help."

"George, that's not the way they treat you, and you

know it." Jenny had grown to like the Seldens, who were neither surprised nor dashed by her Oriental appearance. They had helped to make her stay at the Cape pleasant, and even though George might be joking she chided him.

"Anyway, isn't it dandy? We have the whole day!"

There was an emphasis on the plural pronoun that made Jenny say, "We have a guest, a boy from Kansas City. Alan Carlisle."

"Oh?" George's face fell and he glanced toward the steps.

"He'll be along in a minute with Dick."

As though they were responding to an offstage cue, the two boys appeared at the head of the steps a second after Jenny had finished speaking. They were almost the same height, one dark, one fair, Dick too thin and fine drawn, while Alan, by contrast, was robust and full of vigor, with the sort of physique Jenny had previously seen only in advertisements.

George stood looking at the pair as they came running down the steps and across the sand. Dick introduced Alan, inquired, "What are you doing off duty at this time of day?" then quite naturally included George in their group.

If Jenny would have preferred it otherwise, she was too polite to allow her feelings to show. For his part, Alan seemed delighted to have some masculine companionship. "I've been stuck with Janet and a parcel of girl cousins," he explained to Jenny. "Haven't talked to another boy in a couple of weeks."

But you came to see me! Jenny wanted to cry. She

had looked forward so ardently to seeing Alan that she had expected him to have the same longing, and here he was happily comparing notes with Dick and George on colleges and exchanging views on the availability of Wellesley and Smith to Harvard and Williams. Jenny spread her towel on the sand and sat down on it, trying to listen patiently, but seething internally. All of her expectations seemed to be going astray.

She scooped up a handful of sand and let it run like granulated sugar between her fingers, feeling as she did so that these were truly the sands of time. Half an hour passed, and the boys were still talking, consulting George Yamada now on the merits of coeducational institutions on the West Coast. Alan and Dick both seemed to respect the nisei's opinions on U.C.L.A. and Stanford, but they were only names to Jenny, and she stifled a yawn, letting her eyes roam to the inviting water and wondering whether, if she were to get up and go swimming, the boys would follow her.

But perhaps that would be impolite. Japanese good manners decreed that she must wait quietly until the men finished talking. George was explaining his ambition to do graduate work at M.I.T., and suddenly he seemed to Jenny much older than the other two. He was more purposeful, more serious, and he spoke with a measured authority Dick and Alan seemed to recognize.

Yet it was George who broke up the conversation,

getting to his feet and holding his hand out to Jenny. "Come on, let's go for a swim!"

His eyes were dark and filled with affection, but it was to Alan's sea-blue eyes that Jenny Kimura turned. She allowed George to help her to her feet, but then inconspicuously and gently pulled her hand away and bent to pick up her cap. As she was pulling it on, out of the corner of her eye she saw a girl's figure flying down the steps. It was Eileen King, vivid as a butterfly in a blue bikini, and she ran over to the group on the sand in spontaneous delight. "What luck to find you here!" she cried. "I was afraid I'd have to go swimming alone."

Alan was introduced, and Eileen greeted him gaily, then ran straight out into the water, plunging into its icy embrace in a manner the boys felt compelled to imitate. Only Jenny waded in slowly, shivering a little as she always did before she got wet all over. Alan might have waited for me, she thought, as she saw his wheat-colored head appear, out past the moored fishing boats, close to Eileen's. Then she scolded herself for being provoked. After all, he'd only followed Dick's lead.

The tide had just turned, and the cold water of the Atlantic was rushing into the cut, so nobody stayed in long. "Let's play some beach tennis," Eileen proposed energetically, as soon as she had dried her short brown hair with Jenny's towel. "Anybody got a ball?"

Dick had one back at the cottage and went to fetch it, while Alan came over and stood beside Jenny.

"You're swimming really well now!" he complimented her.

"I can water-ski a little, too," said Jenny.

"Can you?" He seemed more indulgent than impressed, smiling down at her as though she were a precocious child.

I'd like to show him, Jenny thought, but unless George Yamada could borrow the Seldens' boat the opportunity would not present itself. Besides, she could scarcely talk seriously or any other way to Alan from the end of a tow rope, and it was to talk with him alone that she wanted more than anything else in the world.

In the first place she must apologize for losing her temper on that unhappy night in Kansas City. She must make him see that her anger had been momentary, and that she was capable of understanding his mother's attitude. There were so many important things to discuss that each passing minute seemed golden. "Would you like to take a walk on the beach?" she gathered courage to ask. "It's quite beautiful up around the point."

Alan was about to agree when Eileen came over with five strands of beach grass in her hand. "Let's draw for partners," she proposed. "We'll have a tournament."

Now is the time, Jenny thought, for Alan to explain that we're going walking, but instead he hesitated, glancing first at Jenny and then at Eileen's outstretched hand.

"Come on!" Eileen urged him, smiling persuasively.

Jenny wasn't really surprised when Alan gave a slight shrug and drew forth one of the lengths of grass. Eileen had a contagious vitality that seemed to communicate itself to every boy she met. But Jenny did think Alan might have shown a little more spunk, because it was obvious, even though he promised, "We can walk later," that the tournament would last until it was time for lunch.

As it happened, Eileen and Alan were the two winners, playing off the match while Jenny Kimura sat between her cousin and George Yamada on the sidelines. Eileen was no mean opponent, and Alan had to play for all he was worth in order to beat her. Here is one girl, thought Jenny, who doesn't go along with Grandmother's belief that it is unwise to best a man in a sport.

Yet Alan seemed to be enjoying himself hugely. His utter absorption in the game excluded Jenny, as it did everything but his opponent and the ball. In these moments he seemed a magnificent young creature bathed in sunlight and filled with fire. But he also seemed like a stranger, a person Jenny had brushed in passing, but whom she had never really known.

She found herself filled with an urgency to make him look at her, to break through his bemusement with this beach game and this vivid girl. Her Japanese upbringing warned her to be patient and serene, that this was her nature and her proper mode of conduct, but her experience in the United States counseled her to fight for the attention of her own guest!

The beach hat Jenny was wearing concealed the stormy conflict in her eyes, and long ago she had learned to make her face a smooth mask for her emotions. But she was fuming nevertheless, in a very American sort of way, and when she clapped her hands and congratulated Alan on his eventual victory she felt as though she was being a hypocrite.

Gathering up towels and sunglasses, preparatory to going up to the inn for lunch, everyone else seemed relaxed and happy. "Any chance we can borrow the Seldens' boat and go skiing this afternoon?" Dick asked George, and Jenny's spirits dropped to a new low. Not again!

She glanced at Alan beseechingly, but he was listening to George's reply. "If we buy them a tank of gas I'm sure they won't mind."

"I'll contribute a buck," Dick offered.

"Me too," Alan echoed, oblivious to Jenny's mute appeal.

The boys arranged to meet again on the beach at two o'clock, which allowed barely an hour to change, lunch, and change back into bathing suits again. It became quite clear that the day, as Jenny had envisioned it, was lost to her. She was sick at heart, but she couldn't show it. She couldn't let Alan know she cared so much!

In any event, Jenny thought, although she was a neophyte at beach tennis, she could prove to Alan that she had learned to water-ski with style. This was a small ray of comfort, but it was better than nothing. And her performance might even redeem, to some extent, the ruined day.

✿ FIFTEEN

If Jenny Kimura was unusually quiet at lunch neither Alan nor Dick seemed to notice. They apparently had lots to talk about, including such diverse topics as classical records, the Peace Corps, New England ski resorts, and compulsory military training.

It was boy talk, Jenny told herself, and very interesting, but she did wish that once in a while they would include her in the conversation. She felt as though she were fading away, like the Cheshire cat in *Alice in Wonderland,* and that any moment now she might become invisible.

It was a relief when Mrs. Smith approached the table, as the young people were about midway through their meal. The two boys broke off to get up and see that she was seated. "It's nice to have you here, Alan," Jenny's grandmother said as she shook hands. There was a shade of coolness in her manner, which told the Kansas City lad that he was welcome but that she was not unaware of the rift in his relationship with her granddaughter.

The way Americans managed such social complications always took Jenny aback. Her grandmother seemed very brusque by comparison to her own mother, who would have been just as firm but not nearly so obvious.

Alan, however, seemed to understand the interchange perfectly, and if he was offended he was a master at the art of dissimulation. He smiled ingratiatingly at Mrs. Smith, complimented her on her trim appearance, and said, "I wish my mother would take up golf."

Dessert was served, and Jenny's grandmother suggested, "You children run along when you're ready. I'll open my mail and dawdle over my iced coffee." She sent them off genially, and when Jenny turned to look back she was seated with her head bent over a stack of envelopes.

Emerging once more into the strong Cape Cod sun, Jenny suddenly felt very tired. She wished that she could go sit in the shade somewhere with Alan, or even lie under a beach umbrella; the idea of waterskiing didn't appeal to her at all. Stifling a yawn, she squinted up at the blazing blue of the sky and hoped that the boys were feeling equally lethargic and that they'd call the whole thing off, but the reverse was true.

"Come on, lazybones," her cousin prodded, teasing but affectionate. "You can take a nap tomorrow.

Today is one in a million. We've got the boat all to ourselves!"

Jenny knew that Dick was referring indirectly to the Selden boys, whom he considered at precisely the right ages to have special nuisance value. She couldn't resist the persuasiveness in his voice or Alan's quick retort. "Don't worry about Jenny. She's promised to show me how well she can ski. Haven't you, my little chickadee?"

Why did such an absurd sobriquet touch Jenny's heartstrings? Why did she blush and smile shyly and glance up from under her thick lashes, nodding her head? Why did she want to excel, to top any performance Eileen King might manage? In Tokyo Jenny would have scorned a girl with such overweening ambition, but here. . . .

Here her world had turned topsy-turvy. She was expected to be a different person, more dynamic, more self-assured. And she wanted to measure up to these new standards. She wanted to appear as American as she sometimes felt.

"The best of two worlds," her father had said. "We have the best of two worlds, Middy and you and I." It was true, Jenny knew, but somehow it wasn't enough just to feel the truth in her bones. She had to prove it. She had to prove it to Alan Carlisle.

George Yamada and Eileen were both on the beach before Jenny and her party. Eileen was now wearing a scarlet one-piece wool suit that made her look like a tanager, while George still had on the same paint-stained trunks he had worn during the morning. They were launching the skiff, pushing it down past the tide line into the shallow water, where they climbed aboard.

George, rowing, looked back and waved. "We'll bring the Bristol in," he called, indicating a motorboat swaying on its moorings. Dick waved that he understood, then lowered his water skis to the sand and started to uncoil a tangled line, tossing an end to Alan Carlisle.

Jenny, once more left to her own devices, walked down to the water's edge and tested the temperature with a bare foot. It was still cold, but not quite so paralyzing as before lunch. Besides, on skis she'd be warmed by the sun and only cooled, not chilled, by the water's spray.

Out at the mooring, George and Eileen were making the skiff fast and pulling out life preservers from a compartment up forward. George worked quickly and competently around the boat, and within a few minutes he had the outboard down and the engine running. Steering in a broad half-moon curve, he brought the Bristol smoothly in to the shallow water near the inn's beach.

Dick waded out and secured the tow rope to the two cleats in the stern, then payed it out into the water while George idled the engine just offshore. "Come on, Jenny, you go first!" her cousin called, but Jenny shook her head in protest. "Oh no, please, Dick. Let Eileen. Or you."

"I'll ride along in the boat while you ski," Eileen

shouted to Dick over the roar of the motor. "I'm so full of lunch I'd sink."

"O.K. then." Dick came back to the beach for the single slalom ski on which he was expert, and while Jenny sat gratefully down on the sand, alone at last with Alan, her cousin signaled his readiness to take off.

As always, the sport was fun to watch. Looking light as a feather on the end of the almost invisible rope, Dick soared out of the water and leaned back against the sudden pull, his body arrow-straight, his slimness lending elegance to his skill.

"He's beautiful, isn't he?" Jenny breathed.

Alan glanced down at her. "I told you once you were quaint. You haven't changed," he said.

"I must not say a boy is beautiful?"

"You say anything you like—to me."

So quickly, so instantaneously, Jenny thought, we are back on the old basis! Her heart leaped and she dared to say, "Alan, I've wanted to tell you I'm sorry I lost my temper that last night."

Alan shrugged. "Don't be sorry. You had cause."

Jenny shook her head. Picking up a broken shell, she started to trace a design in the sand. "No," she murmured. "It was foolish of me to be angry at your mother. She only did what she thought was right for you."

"It isn't right for me," Alan muttered. "She can't run my life."

"Have you talked to her about it?" Jenny asked timidly.

"Hah!"

197

"You should try," Jenny said. "You should try to explain that I am not a scheming female." Suddenly she chuckled. "That I only want you for a friend."

"That's not very complimentary," Alan protested. "Also, I hope it's not entirely true."

Jenny Kimura had the grace to blush. "Well—" She hesitated, then unexpectedly buried her face in her hands. "Oh, Alan," she cried in a muffled voice, "please don't tease me. I have none of the experience of American girls in these things."

"Come, come! You mean you've never had a boy friend? Sweet sixteen and never been kissed?"

Jenny didn't realize that this was a rhetorical question. Shyly she said, "I haven't, actually. In Japan only engaged girls—" Then she stopped short, because Alan looked surprised, then embarrassed and touched.

"Forgive me," he begged gently. "I won't tease you anymore, cross my heart." He paused a minute. "I'd almost forgotten how different you are—how unspoiled."

Was this a compliment? Jenny couldn't be sure. She turned her head and looked out toward the Bristol, which seemed in the distance no bigger than a bird dragging its feet in the water, making a creamy wake that concealed her cousin Dick. A breeze was rising, and the bay was ruffled with short white collars of foam, among which the moored boats danced rhythmically. Two children, carrying buckets, were walking along the tide's edge looking for treasures. It was one of those instants in time that seemed haloed. Even if we can't keep seeing each other, Jenny thought, I'll never forget this moment, this day.

The thought trembled in her consciousness, then became too sad to be borne. "You've *got* to talk to your mother!" she insisted with some of her grandmother's authority. "Please, Alan. Promise me."

But Alan refused to make any commitment. "Let's not be serious," he begged. "Let's not look ahead." He sprang to his feet and pulled Jenny up to stand beside him, hand in hand, watching the Bristol swing back to its takeoff point. Jenny felt weak and very feminine as she thrilled to the warmth of his touch. She became a captive, no longer a general who could hope to command.

"You next?" Alan asked, as Dick let go of the tow rope and rode, free skiing, right up on the sand. But Jenny felt overwhelmed by emotion. She needed a while to savor the past fifteen minutes. "You go, please," she said, bowing slightly and spreading her hands, palms upward, in a gesture of deference.

Alan didn't need further persuasion. He was almost as good a skier as Dick, although his stocky figure didn't show up to the same advantage. While Jenny's cousin had bent and dipped and jumped the rolling wake with the lightness of a feather, Alan seemed to meet the challenge of the sport head on, with the forcefulness of a football player.

This made Jenny laugh. "I can certainly see which of you has been living close to the sea all his life," she said to Dick.

"Don't be critical. Alan's great."

"Of course he's great, but you are the better skier, Dick," Jenny persisted. "It doesn't mean I think less of Alan because of it."

"Oho!" Dick exclaimed. "That's in the nature of an admission. I thought you had a thing for this boy."

"A—thing?"

"Slang, Cousin. I mean an attachment."

"I like him," said Jenny primly. "He was very nice to me in Kansas City."

"George Yamada has been very nice to you on Cape Cod, but you don't go all starry-eyed."

"Now, Dick," Jenny hedged, "you sound defensive."

"I am, a little," Dick admitted with a frown. "George is a swell boy."

"So is Alan," murmured Jenny.

"Sure, sure," her cousin responded, "but if it came to a pinch, I'd still put my money on George."

"Why?" Jenny flashed. "Why do you say a thing like that? You scarcely know Alan."

"Granted," Dick returned, "but I'd be willing to bet George Yamada has more guts."

"That's the silliest thing I've ever heard!" Jenny fumed. "You haven't a thing to base such a remark on, Dick Harrington!"

"No, I haven't," Dick confessed with a grin. "I was only trying to get your goat actually. Still, there was something about the way Alan mapped that retreat from Waterloo. . . ."

Jenny swung around angrily and Dick pretended to duck, laughing at her. She met his eyes and managed a smile. "If you weren't my cousin I'd—"

"You'd what? You'd whack me?"

Honesty compelled Jenny Kimura to shake her head. "No," she said childishly, "but I'd never speak to you again."

Once more she turned her gaze on Alan, chunky and solid at the end of the rope, swinging wide from the boat and signaling George to take him back to the beach. "I don't want to be a pig," he said, as he stepped out of the skis just short of the tide line. "Come on, Jenny, your turn."

But Jenny again politely deferred to another member of the group, and this time Eileen jumped into the water and George turned the Bristol over to Dick to handle while he rode along as crew. Jenny began to anticipate another tête-à-tête on the beach with Alan, but Eileen called out, "We've got an extra tow rope. Come on, Alan, let's ski together. It's lots of fun!"

Alan shook his head. "George, you go with her. I'll climb aboard as ballast for Dick—unless Jenny wants to go."

"No, I'll stay here," Jenny called back. After all, it would be her turn next.

She squinted against the sun, then shaded her eyes with her hands as she watched Eileen and George Yamada try to get on balance for a joint takeoff. George missed on the first try, but on the second they were up and away, testing the pull of the ropes, which had a different tension when two people were skiing. They soon felt secure, and as Jenny watched enthralled the pair started to streak out and then in, moving with a swing that allowed Eileen to duck under George's tow rope and fly away on the other side.

The speed and precision seemed effortless, and Jenny gasped in admiration. She had never skied double, but it looked so easy she knew she could do it, especially if Alan were beside her. Clasping her hands, she began to hope that someone would suggest it. What enormous fun!

In her imagination she was already out on the water. With each bend of Eileen's graceful body, Jenny bent too. She soared across the bay, her hair flying in the breeze, her eyes sparkling. Yes, she resolved, today I'll ski without a cap, like the American girls! And tomorrow, she decided, I'll ask Grandmother to buy me a new bathing suit, a white one, very plain, like Eileen's red one. My hair will look black and glossy, and my tan will be more effective. Suppose I am dark? I should make the most of it!

Dreaming, Jenny rocked back and forth ever so slightly. Then, alone on the beach, she instinctively squatted, as Japanese do when they are waiting for buses or railroad trains. She got to her feet again when the boat turned landward, but for a time she had been so absorbed in reflection that she had reacted involuntarily.

The first thing Alan said when he came within hearing distance and could shout over the throttled motor was, "Jenny, come on now! We've got to try this."

The second after he spoke he made a shallow dive from the boat, and Jenny went toward him willingly, wading into the water without flinching at its chill, laughing when Eileen came to help her pick up the bar of the tow rope. "If I can just get up—" she murmured without fear.

"You will. The balance is a little different, that's all. There's apt to be a little more drag."

Alan, a few feet away, was bending to adjust a ski underwater. "If you feel yourself going, let go, that's all!" he called, as he straightened and tested the security of the rubber stirrups. "All set?"

After a few minutes Jenny smiled and nodded. She was crouching, waist-deep, in the cold water, her hands gripping the tow bar tightly, her leg muscles flexed and strong. She and Alan rose as one, smoothly, quickly. They smiled across at each other as they leaned back on their ropes and skimmed off across the dancing water, well out from the moored boats that hugged the shore.

Dick was running the Bristol now, Eileen and George Yamada having been left on the beach. He steered clear of the bars and and made for the long reach to the ocean, keeping well into the channel and racing past the buoys that marked its course.

Jenny laughed aloud in sheer delight. She felt like a paper airplane, weightless, borne on the crest of the water as though she were riding a cloud. Using his body as a rudder, Alan planed toward her, and like a ballet dancer responding to a partner Jenny Kimura answered his unspoken signal and skied toward him, bending her neck as though in obeisance as Alan raised his arms and carried the rope high above her head.

They crossed and recrossed one another's wake,

playing like a pair of dolphins, and as the boat swung back toward the beach it seemed to Jenny that the movement of their bodies was as smooth and effortless as the flight of one of the terns that wheeled above her head.

A commercial fishing smack came toward them, chugging up the channel, and Dick turned the Bristol out of its path, then sportively roared back across its wake. At the same moment Jenny glanced toward the beach, spotting the figure of her grandmother, easily identifiable because of a knee-length beach coat, as she stood poised halfway down the steps.

Can she see me? Jenny wondered. Oh, I do hope she can see me! She raised an arm to wave, and at the same moment her skis hit the fishing boat's roiling wake. Had she been alert, it would have been easy to lift the skis' points and go up and over, but Jenny was off guard. The oncoming wave seemed as dense as a stone wall, and the tow rope was nearly wrenched out of her grasp. As she felt herself falling Jenny succumbed to sheer panic and clung on, forgetting Alan's instructions.

She hit the surface face down, water rushing into her nostrils and mouth. Too late, her frenzied hand released its clutch. The tow rope, riderless, slithered over the whitecapped channel like a snake, and the boat veered to the right. Alan, caught in a cloud of spray as he jumped the manufactured waves, did not see what had happened until Jenny, seized by the current, was far away.

The fishing boat, passing the line of moored pleasure

craft, hid the skiers for several seconds from the view of the watchers on the beach. A shout alerted them to the mishap, and even then Eileen was inclined to treat it casually. "Don't worry," she advised. "We all take a spill once in a while. She'll float around or hold on to a ski until Dick comes back to pick her up."

But George was alarmed. Wading into the water, he tried to discern Jenny's head bobbing among the whitecaps, but only a red ski, floating free, was to be seen. Suddenly frightened, he plunged in and swam toward the channel with a strong crawl. At the same moment Dick swung the Bristol around in a tight curve and started back.

Meanwhile, Jenny was fighting to get up into the air. The breath had been knocked out of her as her chest hit the hard surface of the water. Her lungs had filled with the briny liquid and her head felt as if it would burst.

Flailing around with her arms and legs, she kept her eyes open in the murky green light beneath the surface, but she couldn't seem to push herself up to the top. For a moment her nose burst free of the water, but before she could catch a breath she had sunk again, and now her body was as heavy as a stone. I'm drowning, she thought quite rationally in spite of her terror. I'm drowning and there's nothing I can do about it, nothing I can do at all.

Yet the instinct for survival was great. She continued to fight, continued to kick her feet and flail her arms as long as she had any strength left. Hours passed—or were they minutes, seconds? Jenny's long hair floated out from her head like seaweed, and her will weakened. She was utterly exhausted, utterly spent.

Then, with a shock that brought her back to sensibility for an instant, she felt a tug on her hair. Something, or someone—it didn't matter—was pulling it out by the roots. Once again Jenny gasped for breath, but she only managed to swallow still more of the ocean, which had closed over her head.

❀ SIXTEEN

Jenny Kimura lay very still, her head propped on a pair of smooth white pillows, her eyes closed. There were beads of perspiration on her upper lip and her hair was damp and sticky with salt water. Her legs and arms felt heavy, her head ached, and her throat rasped like sandpaper when she tried to swallow, but she was alive.

A miracle, her grandmother said. Jenny's rescue had been a miracle. Out of the nausea and pain of returning consciousness, Jenny could remember only this one word. How long they had worked over her on the beach, giving her artificial respiration, Jenny would never know. Mercifully, yesterday was no more than a bad dream, and today, the doctor had ordered, she must remain in bed. Rest was always prescribed as a treatment for shock, and Jenny was a willing patient. She had no desire to move or even to open her eyes.

But the sun was high, and eventually someone tip-toed into the room through the door, which had cautiously been left ajar. "Jenny? Jenny dear, are you awake?" Mrs. Smith's voice was hushed, her expression still full of concern as she came toward the bed with a breakfast tray. "I've brought you a glass of orange juice, and some toast and milk."

Jenny made the required effort and blinked against the sudden sunlight. "Thank you, Grandmother," she murmured, and put the flat of her palms against the bottom bed sheet, hoisting herself to a higher position on the pillows.

Mrs. Smith placed the tray carefully across her granddaughter's knees, and suggested, "Just eat as much as you want."

To Jenny's surprise, the orange juice tasted heavenly. She sipped it slowly, letting the cool liquid trickle down her sore throat. But she pushed the toast away and only glanced at the milk. "Maybe after a while," she said.

Dick appeared in the door, dressed in shorts and a knit sport shirt. "How's the invalid?" he asked.

Jenny managed a shaky smile. "Better, thanks."

"Boy, you sure gave us a scare!" he said in a tone of rebuke.

"Sh!" Mrs. Smith cautioned. "Jenny isn't to be bothered. You go away now, Dick. Can't you see the child needs rest, not conversation?" She went toward the open door, waving her hands descriptively. "Scoot!"

Then she fussed around Jenny's bedroom for several minutes, tucking odds and ends into bureau drawers, adjusting the blinds, bringing a chair close to the bed. She took the breakfast tray away, brought a glass of water and a damp washcloth from the bathroom, and began gently bathing her granddaughter's face.

Such ministrations seemed so unnatural that Jenny Kimura smiled again, humor quickening in her eyes. "You don't have to wait on me, Grandmother. I'll be all right." Then, quite without meaning to, she slid down into her pillowed nest once more and fell asleep.

When she awakened the next time, Jenny felt considerably more alert. Once again her grandmother was hovering about, looking anxious, but Dick was nowhere in sight. "Hi," Jenny said.

"It's almost noon," her grandmother responded. "Do you want some lunch?"

"Oh yes!" It was a wonderful surprise to discover hunger approaching. Jenny pulled herself straight up in bed, started to push her hair back from her face, and said, "Ugh! It's full of salt water."

"So were you," her grandmother replied tartly, then smiled. "Good. You look more like yourself."

Jenny nodded. "I ought to apologize," she said after a moment. "I saw you coming down the steps to the beach, and I was waving, when—"

"You don't have to tell me. I know the rest."

"I'm terribly sorry." Weakness made Jenny's eyes fill with tears.

"Sorry? You should be glad! As glad as I am. You had a close call."

"Who pulled me out? Alan?"

Jenny's grandmother sniffed. "Alan? He was half a mile away by the time he knew you'd fallen. George Yamada swam out and held you up until Dick got back with the boat, but by then you'd swallowed half the ocean and then some."

Mrs. Smith collapsed on the chair by Jenny's bed, her back sagging, her hands clasped in her lap. "I didn't think you'd make it," she confessed. "For nearly an hour I didn't think you'd make it, and I promised myself, if you pulled through, that I'd try to be a bigger person, a better grandmother."

"But you're a wonderful grandmother!" Jenny said. She stretched out a hand. "And you've given me a wonderful summer."

"A summer to remember perhaps. But wonderful?" Mrs. Smith shook her head. "I've been a bitter old woman, Jenny, but you've made me love you. Please believe that."

"And I love you too," said Jenny.

Mrs. Smith laughed shortly. "As Pollyanna loved her mean old aunt? In spite of everything?"

Jenny sat bolt upright. "No! Because you're you."

Tears stood, unshed, in Mrs. Smith's eyes. "I remember a letter you sent me," she said, "a month before you came. You had no idea what you were biting off, Jenny, what you'd have to learn to chew. And you wrote, with the most complete innocence, 'My heart is already in your home.'"

Jenny didn't speak, because she didn't quite understand.

"I'm just being overly sentimental," Jenny's grandmother said gruffly. "It's not like me. It's more like your father. Is he still very put out with my attitude, or do you think he'd listen to reason and let bygones be bygones?"

Jenny could scarcely believe her ears. "I think he misses you terribly," she whispered. Then she added, "Oh, Grandy, you'd adore my mother! Truly you would!"

The tears in Mrs. Smith's eyes suddenly overflowed, and she reached for a tissue in the box on the bedside table.

"I'm sorry. I didn't mean—"

"Asinine!" snorted Mrs. Smith, getting up abruptly and blowing her nose. "It's just that you've never called me Grandy before."

"I won't if—"

"Nonsense. I like it. After all, you're just as much my grandchild as Dick."

There was a knock on the door, and a student waitress from the inn appeared with a lunch tray. "I hope I'm not too early—"

"No indeed," said Mrs. Smith, quite unembarrassed. "Please come in."

The girl stood and talked for a few minutes, telling Jenny how glad the rest of the guests were that she was on the mend. "You've made a lot of friends," she said.

"I?" Everyone is being so kind, Jenny thought. They're treating me as though I belonged here, not like a stranger. She listened gratefully while the pretty waitress enumerated the people who had sent their

211

good wishes; then Jenny begged her to thank them sincerely in return.

Gruff and domineering once more, but emotionally shaken, Mrs. Smith insisted that Jenny take another nap after she finished lunch. "Then later this afternoon you can have some visitors," she promised, "if you feel up to it."

"Oh, I'll be fine," Jenny said. "But I ought to wash my hair."

This made her grandmother laugh. "Feminine to the last ditch!" she chortled. "Tomorrow you may wash your hair, but today just pretend you're a treasure from the sea. A mermaid with lank, salty locks. Everyone will understand."

Everyone, Jenny thought when she was left alone once more, might not regard her with the same indulgence as her grandmother; yet she couldn't bring herself to disobey. She dozed for a while, then got a comb and brush and did the best she could with her appearance, tying her heavy hair back from her face with a pale blue ribbon, changing to fresh pajamas, and settling herself high on her pillows once more.

Finding the door ajar, Dick knocked somewhat timidly. "Will I get chased out again?" he asked.

"Oh no! I am very lonely." Jenny smiled. "Come sit down."

Hard on her cousin's heels came George Yamada, rapping at the cottage door softly. "Come on in," Dick invited. "Jenny's recovering. She's fixed her hair."

"But it needs washing," Jenny apologized. "It looks terrible."

"I think it looks lovely," George countered. "Besides, if it weren't for that hair you might not be here. I couldn't get a grip on you anywhere else."

"Saved by the hair of her head," murmured Dick. "Doesn't that make you feel dime-novelish, Jenny my pet?"

But Jenny ignored her cousin's clowning. She held out a hand to George Yamada. "Please, I want to thank you. Grandmother said you were wonderful. If it hadn't been for you—"

The tall young man shook his head, embarrassed. "Dick brought the boat around as soon as he could."

And Alan? Jenny wondered. Where was Alan all this time?

As though she had actually asked the question, Dick answered. "It was a tricky sort of accident," he explained. "Neither Alan nor I could see what had happened for several seconds, and even then we didn't panic. We just thought you'd taken an ordinary spill."

"I'm afraid it was I who panicked," Jenny said. "I forgot the very thing Alan told me, and hung on to the tow bar for dear life!" Even now the memory made her feel shaky, and she let her breath out in a tremulous sigh.

"Don't think about it," George advised sensibly. "It's over and done with, and we all feel very lucky. Let's leave it at that." He came closer to the bed and held out a book he had been carrying. "I brought you something to read."

It was a volume of verse, thin and delicate and easy to hold, and on the flyleaf George had written a quotation from the author: "To a solid sprite," and signed his name.

Jenny was touched. As she thanked him she stroked the cover of the book with a kind of wonder. This was the first present she had ever received from a boy. And it was such a special present somehow, one she could keep forever, that wouldn't fade away like a bunch of flowers. She liked the inscription, subtle yet complimentary, and she was glad that George had signed his full name.

George Yamada. After the boys had left, Jenny lay and looked at the signature, realizing that the writing was strong and mature, like George himself. George Yamada—Jenny Kimura. Both names half American, half Japanese, so similar until one added a surname—Jenny Kimura Smith.

Dreamily, Jenny recalled a game she and Yukari had played when they were children, a name-changing game in which they linked their own names to those of their favorite movie actors. "Yukari Boone," Jenny would say, then they'd giggle together, imagining. "Jenny Newman."

Now the dream jelled into something more tangible. What might it be like someday, to be married to a man like George Yamada, a rising young architect in San Francisco or some other city on the West Coast?

Jenny Smith Yamada. This was no longer the nebulous dream of her childhood. The juxtaposition of names brought her up short, because they seemed improbable somehow. Yet Jenny Carlisle—

She blushed at her own temerity, and vowed to

214

keep her dreams under better control. But Jenny Carlisle, what a beautiful name. Like the song of a lark in a Japanese garden. What a beautiful name!

There was another rap at the cottage door and Jenny called, "Come in," glad to be distracted from such unseemly contemplation. The last person in the world she had expected to see crossed the beam of sunlight on her threshold—Alan Carlisle himself!

Limp with astonishment, Jenny tried to prop herself higher on the pillows, and thrust George's book of poetry under the coverlet. "Why—why—" she stammered foolishly, "where did you drop from?"

"From Bass River, where else?" Bronzed, broad-shouldered, and apologetic, Alan practically filled the doorway. "Jeepers," he blurted out, "I sure was a great help yesterday. I couldn't be sorrier, Jenny, but everything happened too fast."

"Of course!" Jenny's voice was warm and understanding, but she wasn't thinking about the accident. "How did you get here?" she asked.

"I've got the car," replied Alan, not quite achieving the lightness of tone he intended.

"Your mother knows?"

"Yep."

Jenny clasped her hands together tightly. "I mean, she knew you were coming to see me?"

"Yep," said Alan again.

"That took courage," Jenny said with deep sincerity. "Alan, you are very brave."

"Well, I'm here."

"You're here," Jenny said, "and I'm glad!" She held

215

out both hands and Alan came and took them, crushing them together in his strong grasp.

Late that same night a full moon rode over the ocean. Jenny, who had slept too much during the day, could not sleep now. She lay curled on her side, her fingers playing with a strand of hair, her eyes wide open. There was so much to think about!

It was as though doors had opened in her mind, so that she could see everyone about her more clearly. Her grandmother, so brusque on the surface, so soft within. Dick, both cousin and playmate, transmitting some of his desire for learning to her. Will I come back to the United States to college? Jenny wondered. Could I hope to make Wellesley or Radcliffe? Her heart leaped at the very idea.

Dick would be established at Harvard if Jenny returned a year from now. Alan, by then, would be a sophomore at Williams, close enough to come to Boston to see her. And George Yamada—where would George be? On the West Coast or at M.I.T.?

Suddenly Jenny felt anxious. She wanted him to be somewhere close to her—wanted it desperately. She didn't feel romantic about George as she did about Alan, but she couldn't imagine being in New England without him. He was so sensitive, so strong. . . .

The moon seemed to be growing bigger, swimming closer. Jenny shifted her pillow and trembled a little in anticipation. The world was so vast and wonderful, so unexpected and inviting. She wanted to spread her arms and embrace all the people she had grown to love. Somewhere in the marsh grass a bird called—"Bob-white!"—two sharp notes quite different from the trilling of the Japanese lark that had heralded her departure for the United States. Jenny smiled to herself. She had come a long way in these two months, but she still had far to go.

How far? Only the moon could know.

BETTY CAVANNA grew up in Haddonfield, New Jersey, and was graduated from Douglass College, where she majored in journalism. It was during her work for Westminster Press in Philadelphia that she became interested in writing stories herself, and in 1943 she became a full-time writer of books for young people. She holds an honorary membership in Phi Beta Kappa for her outstanding contribution to the field of juvenile literature. In private life Miss Cavanna is Mrs. George Russell Harrison. She and her husband live in Concord, Massachusetts.

木村じぇにい

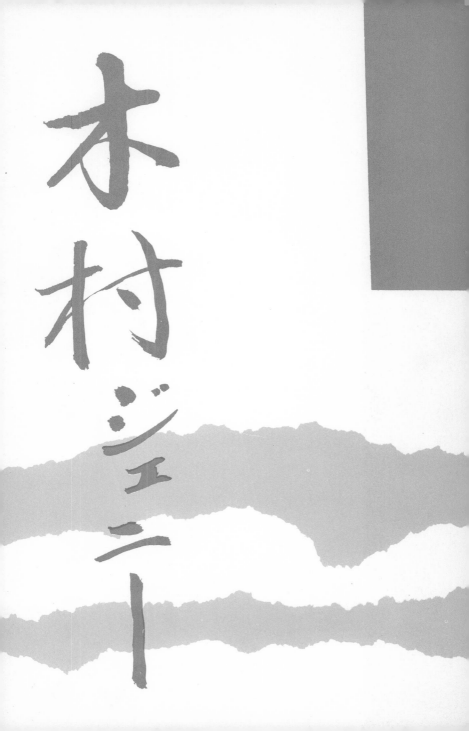

木村ジェニー